WHITE CAVE ESCAPE

Jennifer McGrath Kent

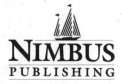

NIMBUS
PUBLISHING

For Beth
and all of the "Taylor's Lane" gang

Nimbus Publishing Limited
PO Box 9166, Halifax, NS   B3K 5M8
(902) 455-4286

Printed and bound in Canada
Design: Kathy Kaulbach, Touchstone Design House
Author photo: Lynne Post

Nimbus Publishing is committed to protecting our natural environment. As part of our efforts, this book is printed on 100% recycled content stock.

Library and Archives Canada Cataloguing in Publication

Kent, Jennifer McGrath
White Cave escape / Jennifer McGrath Kent.
ISBN 978-1-55109-711-4

I. Title.
PS8621.E645W55 2009   jC813'.6   C2008-907172-7

Canada

The Canada Council | Le Conseil des Arts
for the Arts | du Canada

NOVA SCOTIA
Tourism, Culture and Heritage

We acknowledge the financial support of the Government of Canada through the Book Publishing Industry Development Program (BPIDP) and the Canada Council, and of the Province of Nova Scotia through the Department of Tourism, Culture and Heritage for our publishing activities.

TABLE OF CONTENTS

Into the Woods

"Fore!!"

SMACK!

The golf ball went screaming through the air, bounced off a tree, and went whizzing past the ear of a tall, sandy-haired boy.

"Yipes!" yelped Shawn as he ducked. "Tony! Watch where you're hitting that thing!"

"Sorry," said Tony, grinning. "That was my Tiger Woods swing."

"I don't know about 'Tiger,'" said Petra dryly. "But you got the 'woods' part right." She pointed her golf club in the direction the ball had taken— straight into the thick forest of trees edging the Hillsborough Golf Course.

"Oh, *man!*" Tony slapped a palm to his forehead.

"Do you want me to help you look for your ball, Tony?" asked Craig. The younger boy's blue eyes sparked with laughter but he was working hard to keep a straight face.

"Aw, forget it, Craig," said Tony. "We'll never find it in there." He dropped his club into his golf bag with a sigh. "Are we done yet?"

Petra laughed and shook her chestnut-coloured ponytail. "Tony, we're only on the third hole!"

"Just fifteen more to go," said Shawn cheerfully, giving Tony a friendly slap on the back. "Let's go."

"Oh, *man…*"

It was a hot, dry July day, and the four young people were celebrating their summer freedom on the golf course in Hillsborough, a small town nestled between the Petitcodiac River and the thickly forested hills of Albert County. At first glance, they were an unlikely group of friends. Shawn Mahoney was grey-eyed and quiet, with a passion for building and inventing things. Someday, Shawn hoped to design roller coasters…or maybe work for NASA. He hadn't quite decided yet.

Tony, Shawn's classmate and best friend since kindergarten, was as loud as Shawn was quiet. Short and stocky with a bristly brush cut, Tony crackled with energy and had two main hobbies in life: talking and playing video games.

Craig, Shawn's younger brother, took a full-throttle approach to life. He liked vehicles and machines of all kinds. His latest passion was helicopters. Never in his life would Craig forget his thrilling flight in the cockpit of the huge search-and-rescue Cormorant helicopter the previous winter.

And then there was Petra.

Outdoorsy and athletic, she had met the boys just months before, when the four found themselves thrown together in a life-and-death struggle for survival on the Petitcodiac River. On that occasion, Petra's courage and quick action had saved the boys from a fatal plunge into the icy, brown waters of the notorious "Chocolate River." Ever since that adventure, the four friends had been inseparable.

Petra hoisted her golf bag onto her shoulder. "Come on, you guys—let's go." As they set out across the green, a bear-sized dog lurched from his spot under a shady bush and lumbered after them.

"It's great that the golf club gave us permission to bring Hobart onto the course," said Tony, resting his hand on the Newfoundland's huge, square head as they walked along.

"It sure was," agreed Petra. "Hobart has to become familiar with lots of different situations if he's going to be a certified therapy dog. Once Hobie passes the test, Uncle Daryl will be allowed to bring him on real emergency calls, or to visit sick kids in hospitals. *Officially*, I mean," Petra added quickly, as Tony opened his mouth to interrupt. Hobart's last visit to a hospital had been more of an unauthorized break-in, much to the displeasure of the nurses. Petra's Uncle Daryl was a firefighter. Petra hoped to be one herself some day, and hung out with him and Hobie whenever she got the chance.

"Okay," said Tony as he teed up the ball at the next hole. "Prepare to stand in awe...this baby's going all the way."

"Whatever you say, Tiger," said Petra, rolling her eyes.

Craig snorted with laughter.

"Quiet, please!" sniffed Tony. "I need to find my swing." He waggled the club back and forth above the ball. He waggled his behind. He shuffled his feet. He shielded his eyes and squinted in the direction of the hole. Then he waggled the club some more.

"You planning on finding your swing any time soon or should we call in search and rescue?" asked Shawn.

Thunk! went the ball.

Four pairs of eyes followed the ball as it flew up, up, up…

The ball bounced softly onto the green and rolled to a stop just in front of the hole.

"Oh, *yeah!*" whooped Tony. "Just call me Tony the Tiger because I am *GRRRRRR-REAT!*"

Petra laughed. "Get a *GRRRRRRR-RIP*, Hedgehog Head…it was a lucky shot."

"You're just jealous," Tony smirked. "My fans love me."

"Speaking of your fans," said Shawn, "here comes one now…and I think he's about to help himself to a souvenir." He pointed towards the distant green. A small, reddish-brown animal had popped out of the underbrush and was trotting lightly towards Tony's ball.

"A fox!" exclaimed Craig.

Without breaking stride, the fox scooped up the

golf ball in its sharp jaws, scampered across the green, and disappeared into the forest on the far side of the course.

"Looks like you're in the woods again, Tiger," said Petra, grinning.

"What the—hey! That's my lucky ball!" spluttered Tony. Dropping his club on the ground, Tony took off across the golf course at a run. "Come back here, you mangy ball thief!"

"Tony! Where are you going?" called Shawn.

"Come back, Tony! You'll never find him," hollered Craig as Tony began thrashing his way through the trees.

"I suppose we'd better go after him," sighed Shawn.

"Really?" Petra raised her eyebrows. "I vote for drinking lemonade at the clubhouse until he tires himself out."

"Come on—this is Tony we're talking about," Craig reminded her with a grin. "He gets lost in his own backyard."

"Oh, all right," sighed Petra. "Let's go find him." She headed towards the trees.

Shoving their heavy golf bags behind a clump of bushes, the two Mahoney brothers and Petra, closely followed by Hobart, pushed their way into the underbrush.

"Tony! For Pete's sake—where are you?" called Shawn as a branch snapped painfully across his nose.

"Over here!" came Tony's voice.

The others pushed their way through the branches and bushes. They found Tony leaning against a tree trunk, panting. "I'm sure I saw that little ball thief come this way. But where'd he go?"

"There!" said Craig, pointing at a wisp of red fur disappearing behind some bushes. The four friends took off again in hot pursuit, with Hobart lumbering unhurriedly behind. At last, the kids stumbled to a stop, puffing and panting.

"This is ridiculous," said Shawn, wiping the sweat out of his eyes. "We're never going to find the fox in these woods. We've got no way to follow his trail."

"Yeah," said Tony. "Too bad we didn't have a dog to track him for us. Oh wait," he added dryly. "We *do* have a dog." Panting heavily, Hobart strolled belatedly into their midst and flopped down on the ground with a dramatic groan.

Tony looked at Hobart and shook his head. "Look at you," he scolded. "Lying down on the job when there are foxes to be chased. And you call yourself a dog!"

Tongue lolling, Hobart grinned good-naturedly up at the bristly-haired boy…and gave a vigorous shake of his head, spraying Tony head to foot with dog drool.

"Nice," said Tony, wiping a long strand of slobber from one ear. "Thanks a lot."

"Hey," said Shawn, peering through the branches. "I can see something white through those bushes. Maybe it's your golf ball, Tony. The fox probably got tired of carrying it."

Petra was shaking pine needles out of her ponytail. "Well, let's go get it so we can get back. I've had enough of blundering around in the woods for one day. Come on—race you!"

With a snapping of twigs and a rustling of leaves, the four friends burst through the alder thicket and found themselves standing on...nothing! Shawn, Craig, Petra, and Tony tumbled through the air and landed with a thud in a tangled heap at the bottom of a steep embankment.

"Ooooh," groaned Tony. He looked up: "Oh, NO!"

A huge, shaggy shape came crashing out of the bushes above them. Hobart seemed to hang suspended for a split second, all four paws paddling the air. Then gravity kicked in, and the big Newfoundland dropped heavily onto the pile of kids below.

"*Woof*!" said Hobart, shaking his head in surprise at his sudden flight and abrupt landing.

"*Oof*!" came Tony's muffled voice from somewhere beneath the black, furry body.

Shawn raised his head and gazed slowly around.

"Whoa," he said. "What *is* this place?"

The King Quarry

"It's a golf-ball graveyard!" gulped Tony. "The ground is white with them!"

"The only ball around here is *you*, goofball," said Petra, as she struggled to her feet. "Look closer— those white things aren't golf balls. They're rocks."

Tony squirmed out from under Hobart and blinked. "Whoa, you're right. Hey, what *is* this place?"

"I'll tell you what this place is," said Craig. "It's *awesome*!"

The four friends gazed at the strange landscape surrounding them. They were standing in the bottom of a barren and rumpled valley. The ground beneath their feet was littered with broken white rocks. Large bone-coloured boulders lay lumped together in scattered piles. Above them a white cliff, scarred and weathered, hunched its rounded shoulders against the sky. Its lower slope was covered in a scree of white gravel. Scraggly tufts of weeds bristled from the severe cliff face. It reminded Shawn of a shaggy old man with bushy eyebrows and an overgrown beard scowling down at them. Along the top ridge of the cliff, the pointed prongs of fir trees jutted sharply skyward, like the crown of some old storybook king.

At the base of the cliff, the ground rippled unevenly in a series of humps and hollows. Clumps of thistles, asters, burdocks, and wildflowers sprouted out of the white gravel. Winding and dipping through the middle of it all was the faded track of an old dirt road. In its washed-out ruts, chunks of white rock gleamed through the red dirt like bones.

"Creepy," said Shawn.

"Cool!" said Craig. "What an awesome place for mountain bikes! Look at that dip over there—it's like a half-pipe!" He jogged over to the dirt road. Following it up a small hillock, Craig stopped at the top and peered over the edge. On the other side, the track careened down a short but steep incline before rising up over another hump a short distance away. "Oh yeah," Craig called back to the others. "We could get some serious air here."

Shawn looked at Petra. "Do you know where we are?"

Petra nodded, slowly. "I think we just found the King Quarry."

"The what?" said Shawn.

Petra picked up a chunk of the white rock. Kneeling, she scratched it against a flat slab of shale. A bright white line appeared on the grey stone.

"Uh-huh. Just like I thought," she said, tossing the piece of white rock to Tony.

"Neat—chalk!" said Tony, drawing white X's and O's on another grey rock.

Petra shook her head. "Gypsum," she said.

"Gypsies? Where?" said Tony, staring around in surprise. "I didn't know there were gypsies in Hillsborough."

"She said *gypsum*, not gypsies," Shawn laughed. "Gypsum is the stuff they use to make drywall and plaster."

"The hills around here are full of the stuff," said Petra, nodding. "They used to mine it and haul it down to the Petitcodiac to be carried away on ships. But then the company closed down. The gypsum mines and quarries were abandoned."

"Why do they call this place the King Quarry?" Shawn asked, glancing up again at the looming cliff with its spiky crown.

"Because it was the biggest one, I think," said Petra.

"You mean there's more than one gypsum quarry?" interrupted Tony.

"Sure," said Petra. "The woods back here are full of abandoned quarry pits. There are underground mines running all through these hills, too."

Using the white rock, Tony sketched some more white lines on the grey boulder. He stepped back and surveyed his artwork proudly. It was a stick figure of a girl with ponytail.

"Hey, check it out!" he said with a grin. "It's a Petra-glyph!"

Just then, a buzzing noise like a far-off chainsaw ruptured the silence that lay over the valley. It increased rapidly in volume into a snarling, motorized whine. A pheasant erupted from the bushes, squawking in alarm as three ATVs roared out of the forest. Tires skidding on the loose gravel, the vehicles careened over the jumps and bumps in the old road, bucking like broncos. The hoots and jeers of the drivers rose over the noise of their engines.

"Heads up…they're coming this way," Shawn warned in a low voice.

Sure enough, the riders had spotted them. Spinning in tight, gravel-spraying doughnuts, the three ATVs changed course, speeding directly towards Shawn and his friends.

"I've got a bad feeling about this," said Tony, as the machines roared towards them.

"You and me both," said Shawn. He could make out the riders now. Teenagers. High-schoolers…maybe grade eleven or twelve, Shawn guessed. Two were wearing camouflage jackets and pants, and the other, a worn plaid shirt. The grins on their faces weren't the friendly sort. The camo-clad leader crouched lower over his handlebars and revved his engine into a protesting screech. The other two quads fanned out on either side of the lead driver, cutting off any possible avenue of escape.

"Um, they're going to go around us…right?" said Tony in a worried voice. "*Right*?"

But the ATVs kept coming straight at them. Closer. Closer.

"This can't be good," breathed Petra.

The boy on the lead ATV pointed at them, cocking his finger like a pistol. Shawn saw him grin. The ATV accelerated.

Petra reached out as if to grasp Shawn's sleeve.

Then, in a rush of noise and exhaust, the quads were upon them.

Shawn got a whiff of gasoline, saw the mud-spattered headlamp, and glimpsed the metallic glint of braces beneath the sneering upper lip of the lead driver. Instinctively, he flung one arm in front of Petra and the other over his face. He heard Tony yell…and then the ATVs swerved, missing them by mere inches, and spraying them with gravel. Guffawing loudly, the leader flicked something at Petra as he sped past.

"Ow!" she cried, clutching her arm. "You idiots! You…you…" But for once Petra was at a loss for words, speechless with outrage.

Tony tapped her on the shoulder. "Allow me," he said. "I believe the words you're looking for are: YOU BLUBBER-BRAINED BUFFOONS! YOU NEOLITHIC NINCOMPOOPS! YOU MUD-SWILLING, MOLD-MUNCHING MORONIC MOLLUSKS! IF YOU EVER BOTHER US AGAIN WE'LL FEED YOUR BOXER SHORTS TO THE BEAVERS!"

"Yeah—what *he* said," shouted Petra, shaking her fist at the disappearing vehicles. She sighed and turned. "Thanks, Tony," she said.

Tony waved his hand. "Aw, no problem—I have a way with words," he said modestly.

"Are you okay?" Shawn asked Petra.

"Yeah, I guess," said Petra, inspecting a small, angry, red mark on her arm. "What did that lame-brain throw at me, anyway?"

"This," said Tony. He squatted down near the side of the dirt road and pointed at a small yellowish object on the ground.

"A cigarette butt!" exclaimed Shawn angrily.

"Oh, gross me out the door," said Petra in disgust.

"It's still smouldering," observed Tony.

"Stamp it out," ordered Petra. "Everything around here is as dry as matchsticks…a spark is all it would take to send these hills up in smoke."

Tony ground the butt ferociously beneath the heel of his sneaker.

"Come on, guys," said Shawn. "Let's get back to the course. Are you ready, Craig?"

No answer.

"Craig?" Shawn looked around him in alarm. His younger brother was nowhere to be seen.

Shawn shouted again. "*Craig!*"

The white cliffs glowered down at him in obstinate silence. Shawn turned back to Tony and Petra. "Where is he?" he asked.

"And where is Hobart?" said Petra.

A Ghost Underground

"Okay," said Petra, "everybody just stop and think—when was the last time one of us saw Craig or Hobart?"

Shawn ran his hand through his hair, and scanned the impassive cliff face for the hundredth time. "I don't know."

The three of them had dashed about the quarry, searching without success.

"*Think*," insisted Petra. "When was the last time anybody heard Craig say anything?"

"I don't *know*," Shawn said again in frustration.

"What about when the ATVs came?" Tony said. "Craig loves anything with an engine…I can't imagine him keeping quiet about that."

"You're right!" said Shawn. "He can't have been with us when the ATVs showed up or he would have said something for sure." He shook his head angrily. "I thought he was right behind me when the ATVs came. How could I have not noticed that my own brother was missing?" He kicked a rock savagely, sending it bouncing off the stubbly chin of the cliff.

"None of us noticed," Petra said bluntly. "We were

all a little preoccupied with the problem of impending death."

"The half-pipe!" exclaimed Tony, suddenly.

"The what?" said Shawn—but Tony was already running.

"The half-pipe!" Tony called back over his shoulder. "That big dip in the road…Craig said it would be a good place to ride a mountain bike. *That* was the last thing he said." He took off along the dirt road.

When Shawn and Petra caught up with him, Tony was standing at the top of the dip in the road. It did look like a half-pipe.

"This is it," said Tony. "This is the last place I remember seeing Craig."

Petra shaded her eyes with her hand and scanned the quarry again. "We looked over here already," she said, shaking her head. "I still don't see anything."

"CRAIG!" called Shawn.

"HOBART!" yelled Tony.

Nothing.

Shawn strained his ears, listening:

A fat bumblebee hummed quietly to itself as it burrowed busily into the petals of a purple flower. Grasshoppers clicked their wings in a stuttering staccato. A flock of crows cawed accusingly in the distance. And from somewhere beneath their feet, a ghost began to moan.

Oooooooooo-ooooooo…

Tony's bristly hair stood up even straighter than usual.

"D-d-d-did you guys just hear that?" he whispered.

"Uh-huh," Shawn whispered back.

Oooooooooo-ooooooo…

"Petra, do you know what's making that noise?" whispered Shawn. Wide-eyed, Petra shook her head.

Oooooooooo-ooooooo…

The sound came again.

"Aw, I'm sure it's n-n-nothing," quavered Tony. "It's probably just the wind, or a creaking tree trunk, or the ghost of some long-dead miner buried in the gypsum and doomed to haunt the quarry forever."

"Way to make us feel better," said Shawn.

"Don't mention it," said Tony.

Oooooooooo-ooooooo…! the sound moaned from somewhere below them.

"Spare me, O Great Ghost of the Quarry!" cried Tony, falling to his knees.

"Tony, there are no such things as ghosts," hissed Petra.

Oooooooooo-ooooooo…!

"Oh y-y-yeah?" chattered Tony. "Tell that to our p-p-paranormal pal down there." Tony pointed to the ground.

"That's exactly what I intend to do!" huffed Petra. "There must be a logical explanation…" She walked away from the boys, staring hard at the ground.

"Uh, Petra…what are you doing?" asked Shawn warily.

"Looking for our underground ghost," she answered. "That sound has to be coming from somewhere."

Shawn moved cautiously across the quarry floor, kicking at piles of white rubble and pushing aside clumps of scraggly bushes. "And what are we looking for, exactly?"

"Oh, just the usual stuff," Tony interjected before Petra could answer. "You know—gateways to the underworld, portals to alternate universes, rips in the space-time continuum…stuff like that."

"You watch way too much TV," Shawn told him.

"Well, you never know," said Tony seriously, talking over his shoulder as he pushed his way through a patch of tall weeds. "I saw this show on TV last week about UFOs and—"

Tony disappeared.

Shawn blinked. One moment, Tony had been standing in the long grass, a few metres away. The next, he was gone.

"This has got to stop happening," said Petra.

Shawn and Petra sprinted towards the spot where Tony had been standing.

"*Whoa!*" yelled Shawn, skidding to a stop as a gaping hole suddenly appeared at his feet. He teetered, arms flailing, and then Petra's hand was gripping his elbow, yanking him back from the edge.

"It's a sinkhole!" gasped Petra.

Shawn gave a low whistle. "That hole could swallow my dad's car! What made it? A meteor?"

Petra shook her head. "The ground collapsed. Gypsum erodes really easily. So when rain or underground springs wash away a pocket of underground gypsum, there's nothing left to support the soil on top, and the ground sinks in on itself. Kind of like when you dig a hole in a snowbank and the roof caves in. My uncle says there are all kinds of sinkholes back here…and more could open up at any time."

"Hey, stop talking and GET ME OUT OF HERE!" It was Tony's voice, sounding weirdly hollow, and it was coming from the sinkhole. Shawn threw himself on his belly and peered over the edge.

"Tony! Are you okay?"

"I'm okay," came Tony's voice, "considering I'm siting right next to our underground ghost."

In the Hole

Shawn looked down into the sinkhole. The ground had collapsed into a funnel shape; it was like looking down into a big, empty ice-cream cone. The walls of the sinkhole were made of loose, reddish-brown soil, freckled white with bits of gypsum. At the bottom of the pit, Shawn could see Tony staring up at him. Next to Tony loomed a dark, shadowy shape. Before Shawn could say anything, the black shape threw back its head, opened its massive jaws…and howled.

Ooooooooo-ooooooo…! The cone-shaped hole worked like a giant megaphone—the howl rose mournfully, echoing weirdly off the dirt walls.

Tony clapped his hands over his ears and glared at the great black beast sitting next to him. "All right, all right—we heard you already!"

Hobart dropped his head and gave a short, apologetic bark.

"Meet our underground ghost," Tony called up to Shawn, jerking his thumb at the big Newfoundland dog. "And guess what—he's got company." Another shape stirred in the shadows behind Tony and a second face squinted up into the sunlight at Shawn.

"Hey, bro."

It was Craig. His voice sounded shaky and sheepish. "I took a wrong step and ended up down here. And Hobart followed me before I could tell him to stay."

"Lucky for you he did," said Shawn. "He's got a louder voice than you do."

"All right," said Petra, her voice suddenly brisk and businesslike. "Let's get you out of there."

A short search rewarded them with a long, stout stick, which they lowered into the hole. Several minutes later, after much scrambling (and a certain amount of arguing), the "underground ghosts" re-emerged into the sunlight, shoving and pulling one very unhappy Newfoundland dog between them.

"Next time, *you* get the rear end," Tony grumbled at Craig. Tony, who had been pushing Hobart from behind while Craig hauled him up by his collar, was covered in red dirt from the dog's scrabbling paws. "I think he kicked half the hole back down on my head!"

Tony rubbed his sleeve across his face—but since the sleeve was as dirty as his face, it didn't improve matters much.

"We should go somewhere where you can get washed up," said Petra, grinning as Tony blinked at her from a mask of dirt.

"The golf club," said Tony, nodding decisively. He paused to shake an earthworm out of his shorts. "I've had enough of nature for one day. Besides, I think I hear a cheeseburger calling my name."

Picking their way carefully across the quarry floor (and keeping a sharp eye out for sinkholes this time), the friends regained the dirt road and began following its twisting white ruts back towards the golf course. But they had only been walking for a few minutes when a familiar buzzing sound reached their ears. And it was getting louder.

"Uh-oh," said Petra. "The ATVs are coming back."

Tragedy

"ATVs?" said Craig. "Cool! Hey, maybe they'll take us for a ride."

"I don't think you want to ride with these guys," Shawn told him.

The buzzing was getting louder. It was coming from the trail ahead of them, and it was approaching quickly.

"Maybe it's just a really big mosquito," said Tony, hopefully. "A really, *really* big mosquito…"

Petra looked at him and raised her eyebrows.

"Or maybe not," said Tony.

"We should get out of sight," suggested Shawn.

"Over there," said Petra, pointing behind them. The boys followed her gaze. A narrow white footpath veered away from the road, snaking up a steep hill at the back of the quarry to vanish into the forest.

"Good eye," Shawn told her. "Let's go!"

The four friends and Hobart scrambled up the steep path, sneakers (and paws) skidding on the loose, white rock. Reaching the top, they flopped down in the shade of the forest's edge. Shawn crawled forward on his belly and peered back down the way they had come. From up here, he had a perfect view of the quarry. It sprawled across the landscape like a scar—an alien-looking terrain of white boulders, cliffs, sinkholes, and gullies. Tall, straw-like grasses waved above the white rubble. Patches of poplar trees huddled here and there, and stands of stunted spruce sprouted like prickly islands in a hard, white sea. The drone of approaching engines reached a crescendo.

"Here they come," Shawn whispered.

Below them, the same ATVs sped into sight. Revving their engines, the riders zoomed into the quarry, bouncing and careening over the uneven terrain.

"That looks like so much fun," Craig sighed wistfully. "Why can't we just go down and hang out with them for a while?"

"Trust me," Shawn told him. "You don't want to do that."

"Sure I do!" Craig started to argue, but then Petra hissed at them to be quiet.

"Look!" she said.

The noise of the four-wheelers had flushed a deer out of the underbrush. The teen riders gave chase at once, swinging their vehicles around in pursuit. But Shawn noticed something else.

"She's got a fawn," he said.

"Oh no," breathed Petra.

The friends watched helplessly as the ATVs sped after the panic-stricken animals.

Fanning out, they herded the deer before them like sheep, keeping them inside the rocky confines of the quarry, preventing their escape. A large boulder loomed in front of the racing animals, blocking their path. The doe gathered herself for a mighty leap. Sailing over the top of the obstacle, and beyond the reach of the ATVs, she vanished into the safety of the forest. The fawn, too small to make the jump, swerved around the rock instead. Losing sight of its mother, the confused baby veered back towards the centre of the quarry.

Like wolves, two of the ATVs swarmed towards the running fawn. Shawn saw the third rider hesitate… or perhaps his machine had stalled. The fawn was no match for the four-wheelers. The leader pulled up alongside the galloping animal. Gunning the engine, he reached out one hand as if to grab the terrified creature. The fawn swerved violently sideways to evade the rider's grasp…and rocketed at full speed over the edge of a rock-strewn gully.

From their hidden vantage point, Shawn and his friends cried out in horror and dismay.

The fragile fawn tumbled down into the ravine, coming to a violent stop against a rock. It lay motionless, its neck twisted at an unnatural angle.

The chase was over.

Petra covered her face in her hands. "Oh no!" she wept. "Oh no, no, no!" Tony stared at the scene below, his face frozen in shock. Craig jumped up, fists clenched, and started to head down the path toward the ATVs, but Shawn caught up to him and pulled him back roughly. "Stay here!" he choked. "There's nothing we can do now."

Down below, the ATV riders cut their engines and dismounted. They gathered at the top of the little gully, looking down at the lifeless body. A moment of utter silence fell over the quarry. Then the leader raised both his arms over his head...and cheered. After a hesitant second, his buddy copied him, and soon they were exchanging high-fives and slapping each other on the back. The third rider continued to stand over the gully, looking down at the fawn. Finally, the leader pulled a pack of cigarettes out of his pocket and passed them around.

"We've seen enough. Let's go," said Shawn.

Beside him, Craig was shaking his head in disbelief.

"That wasn't cool," he kept saying. "That wasn't cool at *all*."

Petra was still weeping silently, tears of fury and sorrow streaking her cheeks. Shawn touched her shoulder gently and motioned towards the forest.

"We'll go this way for now, and give those guys time to take off. We can double back when they're gone." He got up and headed along the trail into the woods. Petra, Tony, and Craig stumbled after him, with Hobart padding along behind.

The friends walked in silence along the forest trail until they were well out of sight and earshot of the quarry. When they reached a small pocket of sunshine pooling on the track in front of them, they all stopped together, as if by some unspoken signal. Petra simply stood still, staring down at the carpet of leaves and pine needles beneath her feet.

"I can't believe they did that," she said. "I can't *believe* it."

Shawn shook his head. He couldn't believe it either. Even the normally chatty Tony said nothing, but stared bleakly down at the trail.

Suddenly Craig snapped a branch angrily across his knee with a crack that made them all jump.

"I *hate* them," he said, his voice low and fierce. "I hate those guys! I hope they crash their stupid quads and bust them up into little, tiny pieces of scrap metal!"

"We all feel that way, bro," said Shawn quietly. "But we can't change what happened."

"We can report them to the RCMP," said Petra fiercely.

Shawn nodded. "*That* we can do." He glanced at his watch. "I bet those guys are gone by now. It's probably safe to head back."

Shawn led the way back down the trail. His friends followed in glum silence. They had almost reached the quarry when Tony lifted his head and sniffed the air.

"Man, I'm so hungry I can already smell the barbecue back at the club restaurant." He closed his eyes, inhaled, and sighed dreamily: "Mmmmm… cheeseburgers."

Craig wrinkled his nose. "Hmm. Smells more like smoke to me."

"I hope they're not burning the cheeseburgers!" said Tony, opening his eyes in sudden alarm.

"How can you think about food at a time like this?" Petra asked him.

"It's called 'comfort food,'" Tony told her. "Cheeseburgers cheer people up. It's a well-known fact." Petra opened her mouth to reply, but the whine of approaching engines cut their conversation short.

"Oh no!" groaned Petra. "Not these guys again!"

"Let 'em come!" growled Craig, cracking his knuckles.

Just ahead, the trail dropped out of sight into a steep dip. From somewhere down in the hollow came the sound of rubber tires crunching across gravel. The engine noise swelled like a swarm of angry hornets.

"Get off the path!" Shawn barked. He pulled Craig and Tony into the underbrush at the side of the trail. Petra grabbed Hobart's collar and hauled him into the bushes too.

Just in time.

Three ATVs flew over the crest of the hill and slammed down onto the trail, tearing up the ground where Shawn and his friends had been standing just seconds before. The riders weren't laughing now. They were hunched low over their handlebars, gunning their engines, urging their machines forward at breakneck speed. Their mouths were grim, their eyes wide. The first two quads flashed past in a spatter of mud and disappeared around a bend. The third quad was almost out of sight when its driver suddenly slammed on his brakes and skidded to a stop. Twisting around in his seat, the dark-haired teen spat a single word at them:

"*Run!*"

Smoking is Hazardous to Your Health

"Run?" gulped Tony. "Did he say *run*?"

"Run? Why?" wondered Shawn, looking down the empty trail.

"And from what?" asked Petra skeptically, crossing her arms across her chest. "Those bozos probably just heard a porcupine in the bushes and thought it was a bear."

"Please don't use the B-word," groaned Tony, glancing nervously at the dense underbrush.

"What B-word? You mean—b-b-b-*bear*?" Petra teased. She knew how Tony felt about bears. Bears were one of Tony's worst fears (second only to ice floes). Last winter Tony had mistaken Hobart for a bear when the huge, black dog had jumped aboard Petra's boat during that icy river rescue. Hobart and Tony had since become fast friends, but Tony still had nightmares about being sat on by a big, shaggy bear. Petra smirked. "Honestly, Tony, I don't know how you *bear* this bear phobia of yours."

"Funny," growled Tony. "Ha ha."

"Uh, guys? I hate to interrupt, but maybe the ATV kid thought we should run from that thundercloud over there," Craig said, pointing. A low black cloud roiled menacingly, curling into the sky over the quarry.

"Whoa. That wasn't there a few minutes ago," said Shawn.

"I don't think that's a thundercloud," said Petra. She sprinted back to the crest of the hill and looked down. "Uh-oh."

The boys dashed to her side.

The quarry was on fire. A huge bank of smoke was tumbling into the sky like an upside-down avalanche of black snow.

"Those guys with their cigarettes!" exclaimed Shawn. "I'll bet you anything that's what started it!"

The friends stared as flames swept across the dry, scrubby landscape like a tsunami. Shrubs, bushes, and the tall yellow grasses were swallowed in a wave of fire. The wave swelled and spread, sending new ripples of orange flame flowing down into every hollow and crevice. The red-orange wave rushed across the open ground of the quarry. Then, as they watched, it crested and crashed against the forest's edge.

Trees became torches.

The wave of fire became a wall.

Run! Shawn tried to say, but his throat was suddenly so dry it came out as a voiceless whisper. He swallowed. The wall of fire was moving towards them.

"RUN!" This time it came out as a half-strangled sort of squawk.

"But the golf course is on the other side of the fire!" yelped Craig. "We're cut off!"

"Get back into the woods! Go!" yelled Shawn.

"But the woods are on *fire*!" protested Tony.

"Yeah, I noticed!" said Shawn. "But we don't have a lot of options here. Run!"

The four young people whirled and bolted up the trail, deeper into the forest.

"I guess my dad was right," Tony panted as they pounded up the forest path.

"About what?" gasped Shawn.

"Well…my dad… always says…that cigarettes can kill you," puffed Tony as he ran. "But I never thought they would kill me quite this soon. Especially since *I don't smoke*!"

Shawn stole a quick glance behind him. Smoke was boiling into the sky above the quarry like lava from a volcano. It formed a seething, churning cloud whose dark underbelly glowed orange from the flames. Here on the trail, long, ghostly fingers of smoke were already clawing at the friends, reaching for them as if to pull them back into the fiery belly of the beast. Shawn's eyes were stinging. He could feel the smoky fingers wrapping themselves around his throat. The smell fogged his brain, filling him with panic.

The forest fire was gaining on them.

Run, Run as Fast as You Can...

It felt like a nightmare.

Shawn was running through the woods as fast as he could.

Bushes tore at his clothing. Branches lashed his face and hands. He didn't know where he was. He didn't know where he was going. He only knew that he must *run*. The sound of pounding sneakers and ragged breathing filled his ears. He felt, rather than saw, his friends running beside and behind him. The trail flashed past under his feet, sometimes dipping and twisting, as if trying to buck him off. Smaller trails snaked off to the right and left. Shawn ignored these, staying on the widest trail, the path of least resistance. He was panting in painful, whistling gulps now...but the air was laced with smoke, and he couldn't catch his breath.

Then, just ahead, the trail split in two. Shawn veered right, unthinkingly. His friends swung onto the new trail with him, running hard.

No. Not running, Shawn thought suddenly. *Stampeding*. Just like the deer did from the ATV. The realization flashed through Shawn like an electric shock. *We're going to run ourselves to death—*

The ground fell away from beneath his feet. Shawn threw out his hands to catch himself, but nothing was there. He hit a sharply sloped bank with a grunt that forced the last of the air out of his lungs. Then he was rolling over and over, somersaulting, tumbling, until a bone-jarring crash into a tree stump brought him up short.

Everything was dark.

It took a few seconds for Shawn to realize he was lying face down. The cool, moist ground of the forest floor was pressed against his eyelids. He tasted dirt and rotted leaves and something sharp and tangy... blood. Shawn stayed very still while he waited for the world to stop spinning. There was a shout and the sound of skidding sneakers. Then Craig was kneeling beside him, pawing at his shoulder.

"Shawn! Shawn! Are you all right?"

Shawn considered this question carefully. All of his body parts still seemed to be attached.

That's good news, he thought. He tried an experimental wiggle of his fingers and toes. They moved.

Even better.

He lifted his head, gingerly.

Ohhhh...not so good. He spit out a mouthful of leaves and blood.

"Shawn! Can you hear me? Oh, man—you're bleeding! Petra, Shawn's *bleeding*!" Craig's shrill voice reverberated through Shawn's aching skull. Something warm and sticky was gumming up his right eye and running down his cheek.

"Shawn?" It was Petra's voice beside him now. "Don't move until you're sure nothing's broken." Shawn felt her fingers moving lightly and quickly over his arms and legs, checking for fractures. "How's your neck? Is it sore?"

"'Mokay" Shawn mumbled. He pushed himself up into a sitting position just as Tony came sliding down the side of the ravine in a hail of dirt and pine needles.

"Shawn! Buddy! Are you okay? Do you know your name? How many fingers am I holding up?" Tony was waving his hands wildly in front of Shawn's face. Shawn pushed him away weakly.

"Tony," he groaned, "you just *told* me my name... and how am I supposed to see how many fingers you're holding up when you're flapping them around like a chicken with its tail on fire?"

"Yup, he's okay," Tony said with a relieved grin. "Same old Shawn. But, man!" Tony peered into Shawn's face and cringed. "You are messed up!"

Shawn touched his forehead gingerly and winced as his fingers came back red with blood.

"Head wounds bleed a lot," said Petra matter-of-factly as she examined the cut above Shawn's eye. "It looks worse than it is. You'll probably need a couple of stitches, though. In the meantime, put this on it." She dug her fingers into the ground and peeled back a thick square of green moss, about the size of a washcloth. "It'll help stop the bleeding."

Petra pressed the velvety plant gently against Shawn's forehead. The coolness of the moss felt good. Soft. Sort of like Petra's hair where it was brushing against the side of his neck…

"Uh, th-thanks," Shawn stammered, pulling away hastily. "I'm fine. Really."

Silently, Petra handed him the piece of moss and sat back on her heels. She continued to watch him with a worried expression.

"Are you sure you're okay?" Craig asked his brother. "Because you look terrible."

Shawn managed a crooked grin. "Thanks for the compliment. I'll be all right."

"That's optimistic," observed Tony, "considering we're lost in the woods in the middle of a forest fire. Or did that bump on the head make you forget about that small but oh-so-important detail?"

Shawn got slowly to his feet. The ground seemed to tilt slightly and he put a hand on his brother's shoulder to steady himself. "No, I didn't forget. But we need a plan. If we keep running blind, we're going to get ourselves killed. Petra, what do you know about forest fires? Did your Uncle Daryl ever talk about them?"

"Um…" Petra swallowed hard and tried to think. "Well, there are different types of wildfires…"

"That's good," Shawn said encouragingly. "Can you remember what they are?"

"There are ground fires," said Petra, her eyebrows wrinkled together as she struggled to remember. "They smoulder underground feeding on roots and dead leaves and stuff that's in the soil. They're hard to spot and harder to put out. Then there are…um… surface fires. That's what this one is, I think."

"How do they burn?" asked Shawn.

"Fast," said Petra. "Surface fires travel along the top of the ground, burning up grass, bushes, the lower branches of trees—stuff like that. A surface fire can move pretty quickly."

Tony looked nervously over his shoulder. "So, uh, maybe we should be going now? Huh, guys? Let's save the natural science lesson for another time, okay?"

"Then there's the crown fire," continued Petra. "That's the bad one."

"Like this one's *not*?" Tony exclaimed.

"How bad?" asked Shawn.

"Very bad," said Petra. Her face looked tight and strained. "That's when the fire climbs up the trees and leaps from treetop to treetop in seconds. Basically, the forest explodes."

"Okay, then," said Shawn. "Let me get this straight. Ground fires, sneaky. Surface fires, fast. Crown fires, bad."

"*Very* bad," corrected Petra.

"So what kind of fire is this one, again?"

"Who cares?" interrupted Tony, pulling at Shawn's

sleeve. "It's hot. It's fast. It's big and it's getting closer every minute. Let's just go, already!"

"Go where?" Shawn rounded on his friend. "Go where, exactly, Tony? Look where we are!" Shawn threw his arms wide to the forest that surrounded them on all sides. "We don't know where we are! We don't even know where the fire is anymore. What if we run straight into it, huh? What then?"

Tony stared at Shawn. His eyes were wide and frightened. "I don't know," he whispered.

"You're supposed to stay in one spot if you get lost," ventured Craig. "Maybe we should just stay put until somebody comes looking for us."

"Nobody's going to be looking for us for hours," said Petra. "We're supposed to be on the golf course, remember?"

"If we stay in one spot, we're toast," added Tony. "And I do mean that literally."

Shawn rested his throbbing head in his hands. "We can't stay here. The fire's too close. We know that much. But we can't just take off running, either. We need to think!"

"We need to know where the fire is," stated Petra.

"Hey," said Craig suddenly. "I know what to do."

A Cry for Help

"Come on," Craig cried. "We have to get to higher ground."

Tony, Shawn, Petra, and Hobart struggled back up the embankment behind Craig.

"Where's he going?" panted Petra.

Shawn shook his head. "Dunno." He shot a sideways look at Petra. "So how fast do forest fires travel? Did your uncle say?"

Petra shrugged. "It depends on the burning conditions. Wind. How dry things are. Whether it's a coniferous forest or a deciduous forest…"

"Carnivorous forests?" exclaimed Tony, overhearing. "You mean I have to worry about getting attacked by man-eating trees, too?"

"I said *coniferous*, not *carnivorous*," retorted Petra. "Pay attention."

"Oh, right." Tony sighed in relief. "Coniferous. I knew that. Um, what does *coniferous* mean again?"

"Coniferous trees are the ones with the needles. Evergreens. Pine, fir, spruce."

"Coniferous tree equals Christmas tree. Got it," said Tony. "What's *deciduous*?"

"Hardwoods," said Petra. "Trees that lose their leaves in the winter. Maple, birch, poplar...trees like that."

"Uh, just out of curiosity, which one burns faster?" asked Shawn, scrambling over a moss-covered log.

"Coniferous forest burns about five to ten times faster than deciduous forest," Petra said grimly as she struggled up the steep slope.

Behind her, Shawn and Tony stopped climbing. They looked at each other. They looked at the pine, fir, and spruce trees stretching in every direction.

"Great," muttered Tony. "Super. I *knew* I should have stayed in bed today."

They reached the top of the ravine. Now that he was going more slowly, Shawn could see where the spring rains had washed away part of the slope, just below the path. The weakened soil had crumbled beneath his sneakers, sending him on his wild plunge down the bank.

Standing up, Shawn put his sleeve across his mouth and coughed. The smoke was thicker up here. And it was hotter.

In the distance they could hear a roaring sound, like wind from an approaching storm.

"Where's Craig?" coughed Shawn.

"Here!" Craig's voice came from somewhere above their heads. Shawn looked up, squinting through the hazy air. Above him, a tall fir tree began doing the chicken dance.

That's odd, thought Shawn. He tried blinking the smoke out of his eyes, but the tree continued to shimmy and flap its branches. Shawn rubbed his eyes and looked again. The tree threw a sneaker at him.

"Ow!" Shawn yelped as the shoe bounced off his shoulder.

"Oops! Sorry! I lost my sneaker on that last branch." Craig's face popped out from the prickly greenery several metres up the tree.

"Craig! What are you doing up there?" demanded Shawn.

"Petra said we needed to know where the fire was," Craig called down. "So I climbed up here to get a better look."

"Can you see anything?" asked Tony anxiously.

"Just a lot of smoke," answered Craig. "It's kind of everywhere. But it seems to be darkest and thickest over there." He pointed behind them. Petra scratched an arrow into the dirt trail, pointing in the same direction Craig had indicated. "Okay, Craig, that's good. Come on down now," she called.

Petra squatted down on the trail and rested her fingers lightly on the arrow she had drawn. Shawn and Tony crouched beside her.

"Okay," said Petra. "We know the fire is somewhere over there. Now we just have to figure out which way it's moving so we can stay ahead of it." There was a shower of fir needles and Craig landed beside them with a thud.

"The fire will move wherever the wind blows it," said Craig, pulling his sneaker back on.

"So how do we figure out which way the wind is blowing?" asked Tony, coughing and waving his hand at the smoke drifting across his face.

"I know—we'll build a weather vane!" exclaimed Shawn. "It's easy. We made one in science class last year. All we need is a compass, a plastic water bottle, a drinking straw…"

"I left my water bottle in my golf bag," groaned Petra, remembering.

"We'll improvise," Shawn told her. "What else have we got?"

Petra dug through her pockets. "I just have some lip balm, and a souvenir pin from Free Comic Book Day. She sighed and dropped the items back in her pocket. "Nothing very useful, I'm afraid."

"What about you, Craig?" Shawn looked at his brother. Craig held out his hands, displaying his treasures proudly.

"Um, a half-sucked sucker, one bubble-gum wrapper, a paper clip, two marbles, and my loose tooth that fell out this morning, and…oh yeah, my string collection!" Craig fished an untidy ball of string from his back pocket and displayed it proudly. "Cool, huh? I plan to break the world record for the biggest ball of twine." The lopsided tangle of twine in Craig's hand was about the size and colour of a kiwi.

"Looks like you've got a ways to go, little bro," said Shawn.

Craig nodded cheerfully. "Yup. I've got about thirty years to go before it's record-breaking size."

"It's, um, always good to have goals," said Petra, eyeing the dingy bundle of twine dubiously.

"Okay," said Shawn, rubbing his hands together. "Right. Let's make that weather vane."

"Already done," came Tony's voice from behind them.

The others spun around. There stood Tony, holding a fistful of grass. As they watched, he tossed the grass upward. It fluttered through the smoky air and then swooped like a swarm of green insects over Tony's shoulder and down onto the trail behind him. Tony turned and pointed in the direction the grass had blown.

"The wind's blowing that way," he said.

The others gaped. Tony shrugged. "What? That's the way Tiger Woods always does it."

Deflated, Shawn stared at the pieces of grass lying like confetti on the trail. Petra nudged him. "Come on, Einstein. You can build something out of a bubble-gum wrapper and a paper clip later. But right now we have a fire to outrun."

The four friends and Hobart set off down the trail again, but now they went at a steady jog, keeping a lookout for obstacles in the trail. Now and then they paused while Tony tossed another handful of grass into the air to check their direction. The forest stretched on, as thick and impenetrable as ever.

Glancing up through the treetops, Shawn eyed the sky uneasily. Heavy and thick, it crouched over them—a dark, greasy-grey mass, stained with a blood-red glow. It looked like an alien sky, Shawn thought. An alien sky over an alien planet. Even the forest seemed alien and unfamiliar now. No birds sang, no insects buzzed. Trees loomed over them, cloaked in smoke—dark, skeletal, silent beings. They stood like an alien army waiting for a war to begin.

Bits of fluffy, white ash drifted down through the gloom, stinging the backs of their necks and hands. *The Devil's snowflakes*, thought Shawn.

He shuddered and shook himself. This was no time to let his imagination run wild. He could feel the fingers of panic scrabbling at the edges of his mind, trying to find a way in. He swallowed hard to lock out the fear. He realized Tony was speaking.

"The wind is blowing that way," Tony was saying, pointing at a thick tangle of brush and branches. Ahead of them, the trail curved away in the opposite direction.

Shawn glanced at Petra. "What do you think? Follow the wind or follow the trail?"

Petra chewed her lip nervously. "The trail might curve back around into the fire. We could get cut off. But cutting straight through the woods will slow us down. A lot." She shook her head.

The smoke wafted around them.

"We have to get moving," said Shawn. "What's it going to be? Woods or trails?"

"Heads or tails?" asked Tony, shrugging helplessly.

"*WOOF*!" Hobart was suddenly on his feet, staring hard down the path. The kids looked at him in surprise. "*WOOF WOOF*!" Hobart barked again and took a step down the trail. He whined.

"What is it, Hobie?" Petra asked.

"He's saying, *stick to the trail*!" said Tony, pointing down the path. He patted Hobart. "I'm with you, big buddy—the trail it is!"

Tony started to move forward, but Hobart stood motionless and continued staring straight ahead. The fur rose along his back.

"I think he hears something," said Petra uncertainly.

A long, low growl rumbled out of Hobie's chest.

"Whoa, dude!" said Tony, staring at his furry friend in surprise. "I didn't know you could even *do* that!"

"I've never heard him growl before either," said Petra. She followed Hobart's gaze to where the path curved around a corner. "Uh, guys," she whispered. "I think maybe there's something out there."

"Okay, woods it is," said Tony hastily. He spun on his heel and headed away from the trail, towards the bushes.

"Wait!" said Craig suddenly. "Do you hear that?"

A thin, desperate cry shivered through the smoky air: "*Help!*"

"Where's that coming from?" asked Shawn, looking around frantically.

"That way," exclaimed Craig, pointing down the trail in the direction of Hobie's stare.

"Come on!" said Shawn. They sprinted down the path. Just before they reached the corner, Hobart surged forward in an uncharacteristic burst of speed. The big dog hip-checked Shawn as he rushed past, bumping the tall, slim boy off the trail.

"Hobart! What the—?"

But Hobart had already disappeared around the bend in the path, a snarling growl seething through his bared teeth. An instant later, a piercing shriek of terror cut the air.

"Hobart!" screamed Petra.

The friends tore around the corner.

There on the trail was a four-wheeler, lying on its side.

Pinned beneath it was the dark-haired kid from the quarry.

"Help me," he whispered.

Friends and Enemies

"Oh, man, you have *got* to be kidding me," said Tony in disgust.

The kid struggled frantically to pull himself free of the heavy machine.

"Get me out of here!" he cried, reaching out to them. "A bear! It was just here!" The kid rolled a pair of terrified eyes at a clump of trembling alder bushes at the side of the trail. The alders looked dishevelled; broken branches and tattered leaves indicated that something large had just crashed through them.

But Shawn barely glanced at the battered bushes. He thought of the fallen fawn, of the teens' jeering laughter. He felt the sour taste of hate rise like bile in the back of his throat. He stared coldly down at the struggling boy.

"Help me, please!" begged the kid desperately. He twisted and squirmed, trying to pull himself free, but the heavy machine had him pinned.

"Gee, I'd really love to stay and chat," said Tony, sarcasm dripping from his voice. "But I've got places to go, people to see, forest fires to avoid…You know how it is." He stepped deliberately around the wrecked ATV and started walking away. "Come on, guys."

"Wait!" screamed the kid. "Don't leave me here! The fire! The bear!"

Tony walked back to the boy and crouched down by his head. "Let me explain a couple of things to you," he said with exaggerated patience. "First of all, it wasn't a bear. It was a dog. A very big, very black dog…but just a dog."

"No, there *was* a bear, I swear!"

"It was a dog. Trust me," said Tony. "Second of all, we don't associate with murderers of baby animals, so why don't you just ask your pyromaniac friends to help you instead?"

Before the boy could answer, a black shape bounded out of the bushes and onto the trail.

The kid howled and pointed. "Bear!"

"Nope. *Dog*," said Tony, taking Hobart's drooling head in his hands and turning it to show the kid. "See? I told you."

Petra threw her arms around Hobart. "Where *were* you, you goofy dog?" she asked him. But Hobart just whined and glanced uneasily at the forest.

The kid stared at Hobart in bewilderment. "But— but I was sure I saw a bear," he stammered.

"The stress probably made you hallucinate," said Tony. "It happens."

"Yeow!" Craig jumped suddenly as a spark landed on his arm. Another spark landed on a pile of dead leaves by his feet. The leaves started to smoulder. Shawn jumped forward and scuffed out the glowing embers with his sneaker.

"We have to go," he said. "*Now.*"

"Don't leave me!" begged the kid, swatting at a spark that was eating into the ground a few inches from his head.

"Sorry, man. Gotta go," said Tony. He turned and was about to walk away when Shawn reached out and caught hold of his shirt.

"Hey, hands off the fabric, man!" protested Tony. "What's your problem?"

Shawn sighed. "We can't leave him like that, you know."

"Aw, come on—sure we can," argued Tony. "We're in a bit of a hurry, remember? We don't have time to rescue this nose-wipe. Let him help himself—it's what he left us to do."

Petra put a hand on Tony's arm.

"Listen," she said in a low voice. "I don't like this kid any more than you do, but we can't leave him to get caught in the fire. Nobody deserves that." Tony looked skeptical.

"If we leave him behind, we're no better than he is," added Shawn.

Tony let out his breath in a long, noisy sigh. "Oh, for Pete's sake," he groaned, rolling his eyes. "I hate it when you guys are right. Okay, let's get this rescue business over with so we can get out of here."

The three boys grabbed the frame of the ATV. Petra gripped the teenager by his arms, ready to pull.

"Ready?" said Shawn. "One…two…three…*heave*!"

Together, the boys strained to lift the heavy four-wheeler. A spark landed on the teen's plaid shirt. Petra flicked it away. She glanced down at the boy's white face. He stared back at her, his dark eyes wide.

"Don't worry," whispered Petra. "We'll get you out."

"Ugh! It's no good. The thing's too heavy!" grunted Shawn. The boys let go of the quad, panting.

Panic flickered across the trapped boy's face. "You're not giving up, are you?" he asked in a hoarse whisper.

"Trust me—giving up isn't our style," said Shawn, grimly. "Hang on a minute…" He disappeared into the underbrush. A moment later he was back, dragging the slender trunk of a fallen fir. He dropped it with a thud and wiped his sweaty forehead with a grimy hand.

"There's our lever…now we just need a fulcrum."

Tony glanced skyward. "Falcon? What the heck do we need a falcon for?"

"Honestly, Tony, when was the last time you cleaned the wax out of your ears?" sighed Petra, steering him towards a cluster of boulders by the side of the trail.

"What?" said Tony.

"JUST HELP ME MOVE THIS ROCK!" Petra said, prying a large rock loose from the dirt.

"Okay, okay. You don't have to shout," huffed Tony. He helped her roll the rock across the trail. "But I still don't see why we need a falcon."

"*Fulcrum*, not *falcon*," Shawn told him, dropping the tree trunk on top of the rock so it was balanced like an uneven teeter-totter. "See?" He wedged the short end of the teeter-totter under the chassis of the ATV. Then he walked around to the long end.

"All right, guys. Let's try this again."

Craig and Tony took up positions on either side of the log.

"This better work," muttered Tony.

The air around them was getting hotter and smokier. Shawn looked over at Petra.

"Ready?"

"Ready." She tightened her grip on the boy's arms once more. "All we need is a few millimetres."

"Now!" shouted Shawn. The three boys threw themselves on the end of the log. The wood creaked and groaned against the metal frame of the ATV. "Come on," grunted Shawn, pulling down on the log for all he was worth. The machine shifted ever so slightly.

"It's working!" said Petra. She pulled. The kid's body moved—a centimetre. Another centimetre.

"We can't hold it!" yelled Shawn, struggling to keep his grip on the log.

"Hold it! Hold it!" shouted Petra.

The boy's body slid forward a tiny bit more. And then:

"He's clear! We've got him!" cried Petra, tumbling backwards onto the path.

The boys let go of the log and jumped back. The machine settled back onto the trail with a heavy, metallic groan. Tony and Craig collapsed on the ground, panting.

"Get up!" Shawn barked at them. "We can't rest now. We have to get out of here!" His face, streaked with sweat, dirt, and blood, looked fierce and wild in the eerie light that was seeping through the trees. Tony and Craig scrambled hastily to their feet and followed Shawn, who had turned his back on the ATV and was already heading down the trail.

Petra hesitated. She glanced back at the boy standing by his wrecked quad. He was thin. Taller than Shawn, but not by much. Probably not that much older, either, Petra realized. "What's your name, anyway?" she asked.

"Colin," he murmured, staring at the ground. His eyes were dark in his pale face, and the shadows under them gave him a hunted look.

"Can you put weight on that leg, Colin?"

He shrugged. "Sure."

"Petra, come *on*!" hollered Shawn. He and the others were already several metres down the path. Petra glanced from her friends back to Colin. He looked at her with his strange, hollow-looking eyes but said nothing.

"Well, um…bye," said Petra finally. She sprinted towards Shawn, Craig, and Tony.

"Where's Pyro Boy?" Tony asked when Petra had caught up with them. She glanced over her shoulder. Colin was still standing by the ATV.

"I guess he's going to find his own way out," she said shortly. "And his name's Colin, by the way."

"Who cares?" said Tony, but he turned, cupped his hands around his mouth and shouted down the path: "Hey, you! You'd better get away from that ATV. Gas tank plus fire equals big *kaboom*, you know!"

Colin gave no sign of having heard. He stood motionless, a forlorn and lonely figure. Tony shrugged and turned away. "Whatever. Suit yourself, but don't say we didn't warn you."

The four friends ran a few more minutes down the trail, then Petra stopped short.

"Hang on," she said. The others stopped and looked at her questioningly.

"I don't feel right about this," Petra told Shawn. "About just leaving Colin there by himself, I mean."

"Why?" asked Shawn. "We freed him. He can go where he wants now."

"Yeah, let him look after himself," chimed in Craig. "It's his fault we're in this mess in the first place."

"But maybe he's in shock or something," argued Petra. "We should have made him come with us." And with that, she turned and raced back the way they had just come.

"Petra, wait! There's no time!" chorused the boys, running after her.

"Colin!" Petra called as she rounded the corner. She stopped so quickly that Shawn, Craig, and Tony almost piled into her. There was the ATV.

But no Colin.

Lost

"Weird," said Tony, looking around the empty clearing. He shrugged. "Oh well. Let's go."

"But he was just here," protested Petra. "Where did he go?"

"Uh…guys?" It was Craig. He pointed a trembling finger at the ground. "What's *that*?"

Shawn, Tony, and Petra hurried over to look. Pressed deep into the mud beside the ATV was a paw print.

A very big paw print.

"P-p-p-please tell me that's a Hobart track," quavered Tony.

"Way too big for a Hobart track," said Shawn, shaking his head. He knelt down and placed his hand inside the track. The print had a rounded pad and five toes. On the end of each toe was a long, sharp claw. Shawn looked at Petra. Petra looked at Tony.

"Don't say it," Tony begged her. "Please don't say it."

"Bear," said Petra.

Tony gulped. "She said it."

Craig's gaze moved from the fresh paw print to the abandoned ATV, still lying on its side.

"Oh man," he breathed. "You don't suppose

Colin…I mean, the bear was just here and…and now Colin's…*not*."

"You think Bambi Boy is bear bait?" Tony shuddered.

Petra's hand flew to her mouth. "Oh no!"

With a loud snapping of branches a large, brown body sprang out of the underbrush and landed on the trail in front of them.

"GAAAAAAAHHHH!" yelled all four friends.

The deer threw them a look of white-eyed terror and leaped away, vanishing into the forest in a single bound.

Tony clutched his chest. "Oh man," he gasped. "I can see the headline now: 'Twelve-year-old dies of heart attack after being ambushed by white-tailed deer.'"

"Come on!" Shawn urged. "Let's get out of here."

They ran.

But now bear-shaped shadows seemed to lurk behind every bush. Was that a paw with long, cruel claws reaching toward them…or just a gnarled branch? Was that a breeze blowing those leaves…or a bear's hot breath? The trail rippled along the forest floor, caged in by a wall of tall, silent trees. Branches closed over their heads like interlocking fingers, shutting out the sky. The trail was changing.

Knee-deep weeds and ferns now obscured the dirt track. Craig tripped over a dead branch that lay hidden beneath the greenery. Tony stumbled in a rut. The air was hot and close.

"What I would give to have my water bottle right now," moaned Petra. She rubbed the back of her hand across her dry, cracked lips.

"Look!" cried Craig. "Another path." Another trail flowed through the forest, slicing across their own before vanishing again into the trees.

"Maybe that's the way out," said Shawn, leaning against a tree to catch his breath. They swerved off of the overgrown path onto the new trail. But a few minutes later, this track was bisected by yet another path that snuck off into the trees in an entirely different direction.

"Oh, brother," said Craig. "Which way do we go now?"

"Which way is the wind blowing?" panted Petra, holding a stitch in her side.

"Eeny-meeny-miney-mo," said Tony, picking a handful of grass, "please tell us which way to go." He tossed the grass into the air. The green bits fluttered briefly before dropping back down around his feet. "Great," said Tony. "There's no more wind."

"I have no idea where we are anymore," said Petra, shaking her head.

"Or where the fire is," added Shawn uneasily. Smoke wafted around them from all directions like a poisonous fog.

"Let's go this way," said Craig. He turned right, heading down a path with a decisive stride. The others jogged to catch up with him.

"Why this way?" Tony asked him as they ran through the never-ending trees.

Craig shrugged. "I dunno. I'm right-handed."

Another path appeared and skittered out of sight around a mossy knoll, as if teasing them to follow. The kids stumbled to a stop and looked at it in confusion.

Tony groaned.

"It's like being lost in a maze! Which way leads out?"

"Who makes all these paths?" wondered Craig.

Caw-caw-caw!

High above them, a flock of crows flapped overhead, cutting through the smoky air like black arrows. Through the treetops, the black shapes flitted in and out of sight, moving with remarkable speed. Petra stared at them. Suddenly, she jolted to life.

"We'll follow the crows," she yelled. "They'll fly away from the fire, not into it! We can follow them to safety!"

"Petra, wait—" Shawn started to say. But Petra had already bolted into the forest. The boys sprinted after her. They raced pell-mell through the underbrush, crashing through bushes, scrambling up and down banks and gullies, dodging boulders and dead logs. But it was hopeless. The crows were gone. And so was the trail.

"Petra!" Shawn hollered, trying to catch up with the galloping girl. "Forget it! We can't keep up with them. They're gone!" But Petra didn't slow down.

"I can still hear them!" she shouted back over her shoulder. "I can still—"

Shawn saw the danger before she did.

"Petra, STOP!" he roared. He launched himself into a flying football tackle. The impact caught Petra just above the hip. Down they went with a crash that knocked the breath out of both of them.

"What did you do that for?" Petra gasped. She struggled to get to her feet. "We have to follow the birds. We have to find a way *out of here*! We—"

Shawn held up his hand. Silently, he pointed to the ground. Right next to Petra, a gaping, black hole yawned out of the earth. She yelped in surprise and jerked back.

Just then, Craig and Tony caught up, skidding to a stop beside them.

"Holy cow!" exclaimed Tony in horrified amazement, looking at the hole. "Holy cow, that was close!"

Craig edged cautiously forward and looked down. He whistled. "Wow—do you think it goes all the way to China?"

"I don't think I want to find out," replied his brother, getting to his feet and offering a hand to Petra. "Sorry for tackling you so hard," Shawn said as he pulled her upright. "Are you hurt?"

Petra shook her head wordlessly, still staring down into the black emptiness beside her.

Shawn nudged the ground at the mouth of the hole. A clod of dirt and rock crumbled away and fell into the unseen depths. Several heartbeats later, a faint splash echoed up from the darkness.

"Whoa," said Tony.

"How deep would you say that is?" asked Craig.

"Fifteen metres, I guess," said Shawn. "At least."

"What is it?" asked Craig. "It doesn't look like a sinkhole. For one thing, it's kind of…square."

"No," said Petra, finding her voice at last. "It's not a sinkhole. It's a mine shaft. Look." Now they noticed the rotting wooden beams showing through the soil and dirt. Although eroded with time, the walls of the hole were surprisingly regular, and sharply vertical—like an elevator shaft—plunging straight down into the earth.

"Man, don't they know it's dangerous to leave old mining shafts just lying around like that?" exclaimed Tony indignantly. "Somebody could break their neck!"

"Are there more of these holes just, uh, lying around?" asked Craig, looking around nervously.

"I don't know," said Petra with a shudder. "Maybe."

Shawn looked at the mine shaft. "Hmmmm," he said. "I wonder…"

"What?" Tony prodded him. But Shawn shook his head. "Nothing," he said. "I had a crazy idea, but it's too dangerous. Forget it. Come on—let's get out of here."

Huddled close together now, the friends moved through the trees, eyes scanning the forest floor for any signs of holes, shafts, or collapsed tunnels.

"Did you notice there's not so much smoke now?" said Craig after a few minutes.

Shawn nodded. "We must have put a bit of distance between us and the fire. Let's hope we can keep it that way."

At that moment there was a yelp and a splash. Shawn, Petra, and Craig spun around to see Tony thrashing about in a scum-covered bog. Shawn leaped towards his friend and hauled him onto solid ground. Snorting and gasping, Tony shook himself like a dog, spraying water everywhere.

"What happened?!" exclaimed Shawn, trying not to laugh at his bedraggled buddy.

"What does it look like? I fell in a puddle!" spluttered Tony.

"Must have been some puddle!" commented Craig. Tony was soaked from the neck down.

"C-c-c-cold!" chattered Tony. "And d-d-d-deep!"

"Hey, there's another one here," called Petra from a few metres away. She pointed to a small pool of brown water, half-hidden by weeds and low-hanging branches.

"There, too," added Shawn, pointing out another boggy patch, its murky waters camouflaged by a green scum of algae and floating dead leaves.

"They're everywhere," exclaimed Craig, turning in a slow circle. "Where *are* we?"

"Welcome to the Pits of Despair," answered a voice from the shadows.

The Pits of Despair

"Who said that? Who's there?" cried the four young people. They pressed close together, scanning the surrounding trees for the source of the voice. In the muted and shifting light of the forest, a weird and swampy terrain was revealing itself. Arthritic trees— fir, spruce, a few melancholy maples, some scraggly birches—slouched over scattered pools of brackish water. A camouflage pattern of light and shadow lay in shattered pieces across the forest floor. It was hard to tell where the penny-coloured puddles ended and the brown ground began.

"It's me," said the voice.

The friends whirled. There was a rustling in the bushes and a figure stepped into view.

"Colin!" cried Petra. "You're alive! And…and— *unchewed*!"

Colin looked confused. "Huh?"

"The *bear*, man!" exclaimed Tony. "How did you escape? We thought you were bear bait!"

"Bear? But I thought you said there *wasn't* a bear. I left right after you guys. I found another path—but it got too smoky, so I doubled back. Then I heard voices, so I headed this way." Colin eyed Tony's wet clothes. "You should stay out of that water, you know," he said.

"Thanks for the tip," growled Tony, tugging off one wet sneaker and emptying its liquid contents onto the ground.

"Seriously," warned Colin. "They're not just water holes…they're pits."

"Oh, they're the pits, all right," said Tony, squeezing water out of his sock. He squirmed uncomfortably. "Ew…I've got slime in my shorts."

But Petra looked sharply at Colin. "What exactly do you mean by 'pits'?" she asked. Colin waved his hand at the scattered pools.

"These are all pits from the gypsum mines. Sinkholes, collapsed mining tunnels, old mine shafts—that's what these 'puddles' really are, except now they're flooded. It's not exactly the safest place to get lost. That's why they're called the Pits of Despair."

"The Pits of Despair," repeated Tony. "Perfect." He stepped into his sneaker with a noisy squelch. "This day just keeps getting better and better," he muttered.

"So do you know how to get out of here, then?" Petra asked Colin.

Colin ducked his head in embarrassment. "I've read about this place and I've seen it on maps, but this is the first time I've been in this part of the woods. I followed your voices because I was hoping you guys might know the way out." Colin looked around. "By the way, where's your dog?"

"Oh my gosh—*Hobart*!" gasped Petra. "Where is he?"

The friends launched a barrage of whistles and shouts but the only thing that came back was an echo. There was no sign of the big, black dog.

"Oh no," whispered Petra. "Oh no, oh no…"

"He must have gotten separated from us when we left the trail," said Shawn worriedly, scanning the trees.

"What if he fell into a shaft or a sinkhole?" moaned Petra. "What if he runs back into the fire?" She covered her face with her hands. "This is all my fault! If I hadn't taken off after the crows like that…"

"It's nobody's fault," Shawn quickly reassured her.

"Oh, it's *somebody's* fault, all right," growled Tony, glowering at Colin.

Colin's face went stiff and tight. "I didn't start the fire."

"Sure, sure…and you didn't run that fawn to death, either," retorted Tony.

"That wasn't supposed to happen," Colin whispered. His face was suddenly very white. "It was an accident."

"How about that little victory dance you guys did afterwards? The high-fives? The cheers? Were they accidents too?" Petra's voice was icy.

"I didn't—I mean…" Colin was backing away,

shaking his head. "That was Brad. You have to play along with Brad or else…or else…"

"Or else what? You might actually grow a backbone? Or turn into a decent human being?" finished Tony.

Colin gritted his teeth. "You guys don't know what you're talking about. It's complicated. You wouldn't understand…"

"You're right—I *don't* understand," said Shawn. The memory of the crumpled body of the fawn had come rushing back, filling him with white-hot anger. "We didn't ask you to come looking for us, so why don't you just go on back to your friends and leave us alone?"

"Friends? *Friends*?" The outrage in Colin's voice startled them all. "You think those jerks are my *friends*? They left me behind. I wrecked my quad and they didn't even come back to see if I was okay. They left me alone in the middle of a freakin' *forest fire*! They are *not* my friends. They never were." Colin's chest was heaving as if he had just run a race. Petra, Shawn, Tony, and Craig stared at him in shocked silence.

Colin aimed a furious kick at a tree. Then he leaned his head against the trunk, his anger melting into despair. "My stepdad's right—I *am* stupid," he groaned. "I just thought…I thought if I took the four-wheeler out and showed those other guys how cool the quarry was, they'd stop hassling me at school.

I just wanted them to get off my back. None of this was supposed to happen. But now I've messed up everything!"

The four friends looked at the troubled teen. They looked at one another. Then Shawn let out his breath in a noisy sigh and kicked a pebble into the nearest pool. "It's a mess, all right," he agreed. "But seeing as we're in it together, I guess we might as well try and get out of it together. How come you know so much about this place, anyway?"

Colin lifted his head and looked at them uncertainly. Then he began to speak in a quiet, halting voice:

"I come to the quarry whenever my stepdad is home. Which is a lot, since he got laid off at work. He's...not the nicest guy to be around." Colin shot them a quick look from under his shaggy bangs. "It's quiet at the quarry. Sort of peaceful. Mostly, I just sit by myself and *watch* stuff. It's amazing what you can see if you're really quiet." Colin's dark eyes brightened. "I've seen foxes and rabbits and deer. Even saw a lynx once. I know where the pheasant has her nest, too. *Had* her nest," he corrected himself, glancing up at the smoky clouds coiling overhead. Pain and shame choked his voice.

He took a shaky breath and went on. "Mostly I just hang around the main King Quarry, but one time, in gym class, the teacher showed us an orienteering map. It showed every landmark of this whole area—every rock, ditch, and puddle."

"Don't suppose you happen to have that map on you now?" asked Tony hopefully.

But Colin shook his head. "The teacher wouldn't let me take it, but I went back at noon-hour and had a really good look. We're in the Pits of Despair. I'm sure of that much." Colin furrowed his brow, thinking hard. "That means the King Quarry—where we started from—is to the south of us. The golf course is to the east."

"Which means the fire is to the southeast," reasoned Petra. "It started in the quarry and was spreading towards the golf course."

"So we should go west?" wondered Craig.

But Colin shook his head. "Nothing but wilderness that way," he said. "The forest goes on for miles and miles in that direction. We'd just get permanently lost."

Shawn's eyes flickered over the water-filled pits. "What if…" he said slowly.

"What?" asked Petra.

"What if we went *down*?"

"*What*?"

"Think about it," said Shawn, his voice rising in excitement. "These hills are full of underground holes and tunnels. If we could get below ground, we'd be safe from the fire!"

"Oh no," said Tony, throwing up his hands and backing away. "I am *not* going down a fifty-foot mine shaft. No way, no how!"

"For once I have to agree with Tony," said Petra. "Those tunnels are a death trap, Shawn, even if we *could* get down into them. Which we can't. And besides, they're flooded, remember?"

"Um, not all of them," Colin interrupted. "The Pits of Despair are flooded, but the White Caves aren't. Not completely, anyway."

"The what?" chorused the friends.

"The White Caves." Colin's pale cheeks flushed with excitement. "They're gypsum caves, carved out of the ground by the melting glaciers at the end of the ice age. My dad—my *real* dad—took me hiking there once, years ago."

"Where are the White Caves?" Petra demanded.

"North," answered Colin. "They should be only a couple of miles from here. Shawn's idea just might work, if we can find the caves. And if we can outrun the fire."

"Those are two pretty big *ifs*," observed Tony.

"What are we waiting for?" exclaimed Craig. "Let's go! North it is! Onward and downward!"

He took a running step toward the trees. And stopped. "So, uh, which way is north again?"

Colin shrugged. "I don't know. I thought you guys knew," he said.

"We're doomed," said Tony.

An Electrifying Solution

"Hobart! Hobie! Here, boy!" called Petra. But no friendly black dog came lumbering out of the woods. Behind her, Craig and Tony were arguing about which way was north. Shawn walked over to Petra. "No luck?" he said quietly.

"I just hate to go on without him," she whispered, staring into the forest.

"He'll be okay," Shawn told her with a confidence he didn't feel. "Hobie's smart. And he's got a great nose to guide him. He's probably waiting for us back at the golf club right now."

Behind them, the argument was getting louder.

"North!" insisted Tony.

"South!" argued Craig.

"No way—I'm sure that survivor guy on TV said that moss grows on the *north* side of a tree."

"That's dumb," retorted Craig. "Why would moss grow on the north side? Don't plants like warm places? It grows on the south side."

"Oh geez—there's moss growing on *all* sides of this tree!"

"I think I heard somewhere that ants always build

their anthills on the south side of a tree," Colin interjected.

"Oh, great," Tony replied sarcastically. "Now all we have to do is find an anthill and we're saved."

"Hey," protested Colin, "I'm just trying to help. We have a head start on the fire right now, but it's not going to last. We have to make a decision and get moving."

Petra nodded.

"Colin's right," she said. "Fighting isn't going to help us figure out which way north is."

"It's *that* way!" yelled Tony and Craig at the same time, pointing in opposite directions.

Shawn ran his hands through his hair in frustration. "This is crazy. We need a compass."

"Yeah, how come you didn't bring a compass, Petra?" asked Tony accusingly. "I thought your motto was 'always be prepared.'"

"I wasn't planning on getting lost on the golf course!" exclaimed Petra.

"No one ever plans to get lost," said Tony, wagging his finger at her. "Next time, Petra, you should really think ahead before you go charging off into the woods."

"*Me*?" Petra took a step towards Tony, a dangerous glint in her eyes.

"Okay, okay," said Shawn, stepping between them. "I'm sure we can solve this rationally. No violence necessary."

"Not necessary, but oh, so tempting," growled Petra, glaring at Tony. She shoved her hands deep into her pockets. "YEOW!" she yelped.

"WAH! WHERE'STHEBEAR?" yelped Tony, jumping back and looking around frantically.

But Petra was sucking her thumb. "Owww… There's no bear," she told Tony in an irritated tone. "I just stabbed my thumb with a pin, that's all." She pulled out her Free Comic Book Day pin. "Yeesh! It's as sharp as a needle!"

"There's no bear?" asked Tony weakly, slumping against a tree with his hand over his heart.

"No bear," Petra repeated firmly.

Tony let out his breath. "This day is way too tense, man."

But Petra was examining the pin in her hand.

"Sharp as a needle…" she whispered to herself. She looked up at Tony. She stared at him thoughtfully.

"What?" said Tony. "Stop looking at me like that."

Petra was grinning now. "Tony, don't take this the wrong way—but I need your head."

"*WHAT*?! No way!" objected Tony, clamping both hands over his brush cut.

"I only need to borrow it for a minute," wheedled Petra, advancing on him.

"Sorry, I don't loan it out," protested Tony, backing away. "I'm too attached to it. Literally!" He scrambled to hide behind Shawn.

"Help me, Shawn, ol' buddy," he begged. "The

girl's gone batty. Bonkers. Bananas. She's lost her mind and now she wants mine!"

"Um, what *are* you doing, Petra?" asked Shawn, looking both confused and amused as his two best friends circled around and around him, like a cat after a mouse.

"I need…to make…a compass!" Petra grunted, trying to catch Tony in a headlock.

"Not out of me, you don't!" Tony howled, ducking out from under her grasp.

"How are you going to do that?" Shawn asked Petra curiously.

"Don't listen to the crazy girl!" protested Tony. "You might be next!"

Petra grinned at Shawn. "What's a compass made of?" she asked him.

"Not my head!" Tony declared, skipping out of reach to hide behind Craig.

"Uh… a needle that points north, I guess," Shawn answered. "*Magnetic* north, that is," he corrected himself.

"Exactly!" crowed Petra. She pulled the Free Comic Book Day pin out of her pocket. As the boys watched, she snapped the straight pin off its tiny metal hinge and held it up. "Voila! Our needle!"

Colin peered at the tiny pin pinched between Petra's fingers.

"I don't get it—a needle isn't a compass. How's that supposed to show us where north is?"

"Simple," said Petra. "We turn it into an electromagnet."

"Oh, sure—*simple*," repeated Tony, rolling his eyes at Craig and twirling his finger in circles around his ear.

"It *is* simple," Petra insisted. "Haven't you ever played with balloons at a birthday party?"

The boys blinked at her.

"Well, duh," said Tony. "Of course. But what does that have to do with anything?"

"Have you ever stuck a balloon to the wall?"

"Sure," said Tony. "You just rub it on your—" His hands flew to his head. "Oh," he said, looking suddenly sheepish.

Petra waggled the needle at him. "Care to share your magnetic personality?" she asked Tony. "I need to charge this needle with static electricity, and you've got the best hair for it."

"The sacrifices I make for science," Tony grumbled, but he bent his head dutifully. Petra rubbed the tiny sliver of metal briskly back and forth across his short, fuzzy hair until it crackled beneath her fingers.

"That ought to do it," she said, holding up the needle between two fingers like a tiny sword.

"How are you going to get it to point north?" Craig wanted to know.

"Now that we've given the needle a magnetic charge, it will naturally swing north," explained Petra.

"But…where's the rest of the compass?" asked Craig.

"We've got everything we need right here," Petra told him. She knelt down and ran her hands over the ground until she found what she was looking for—a large maple leaf that had fallen from one of the trees. It was dried out and curled up around the edges. She set it carefully down on a flat piece of ground.

Next, Petra hurried over to a cluster of birch trees. She peeled a paper-thin strip of birch bark off one of the trunks. With her fingers, she tore the bark into a small square about the size of a postage stamp. She set the bark down next to the maple leaf and headed over to one of the Pits of Despair.

"Careful!" Shawn warned.

Petra crouched next to the boggy pool and scooped up a handful of water. Cupping it in her hands, she came back and dribbled the water into the maple leaf. The leaf acted like a shallow bowl. The water pooled in its flat, wide centre. Petra waited until the water was still. Then she stretched out on her belly in front of the leaf. Gently, very gently, she laid the tiny square of birch bark on the water. It floated.

"Okay, Tony, heads up," said Petra.

"Why do I feel like somebody's lucky rabbit's foot?" Tony asked, but he squatted down beside her and presented his fuzzy head. Petra gave the needle one more good polish.

Holding her breath, she stretched out her hand and carefully dropped the needle onto the floating piece of birch bark. It balanced there, hovering just above the water's surface on its tiny barge. The boys crowded around for a better look.

"Be careful," Petra warned them. "Don't breathe on the water. We don't want to blow the needle and get a false reading."

In the centre of the leaf, the needle was starting a slow spin. As the young people watched, it swung in a graceful arc as if pulled by an invisible wire.

"Holy smokes, it's working!" breathed Tony wonderingly.

"Cool!" agreed Craig.

"*Smart*," said Colin, looking admiringly at Petra. Shawn cleared his throat loudly. Colin's eyes returned to the leaf.

About eighty degrees into its spin, the needle came to a quivering stop.

Petra sat back on her heels. "That's it," she said. "That's north."

Separated

"Ow!" Tony yelped as a branch whipped back and slapped him across the face. "Holy frosty Fudgsicles, Craig! Watch it!"

The five young people were trotting as quickly as they dared through the boggy terrain. The forest had gone unnaturally quiet. No chirping birds. No buzzing insects. Tendrils of smoke were once again curling around their ears, and the air felt heavy.

"Sorry, Tony," Craig apologized, looking over his shoulder. "I thought you were farther back."

"Not so much," moaned Tony, rubbing the red welt across his cheek.

"Hurry up, you guys," Shawn called anxiously. He moved up beside Colin, who was leading. "Recognize any landmarks yet?" Shawn asked him in a low voice. Colin shook his head. "Not yet. But we've still got a lot of ground to cover."

"And not a lot of time to cover it in," coughed Shawn. His eyes were beginning to water in the smoky haze.

"Pit!" called Petra, pointing out another scum-covered pool, half-hidden by tangled underbrush.

"Watch your step." The five young people picked their way carefully around the innocuous-looking puddle and jogged on through muggy heat. Tony wiped the sweat from his forehead and glanced back at the water.

"Uh, guys?" he called. "How come we can't just wait out the fire in one of these pools? It seems weird to be running from a fire when there's water all around us."

Ahead of him, Petra was already shaking her head. "No good, Tony. When the fire gets here, the air temperature will shoot up hotter than an oven. Air that hot would cook your lungs. If the smoke didn't kill you first, that is."

"Don't you ever have any good news?" Tony complained as he followed her.

When they passed another pool, they paused. Borrowing Petra's stick pin (and Tony's head), Shawn quickly made another compass and checked their direction. "We need to veer a little more to the right," he said, putting the pin in his pocket. They adjusted their course slightly, but had only been hiking for a few minutes when Shawn stopped again.

"Do you guys hear that?"

They halted, listening.

It was coming from behind them: a low, rushing, roaring sound, like waves washing ashore on a rocky beach. The rushing noise became a crackling noise.

And then:

"Fire!" yelled Shawn. The dark shadows pooling beneath the underbrush morphed into smoke. Tentacles of flame flicked out of the foliage. As they watched in horror, the fire divided with serpentine speed, slithering up tree trunks, strangling bushes. Long fingers of flame began crawling across the ground towards them.

"Go go go!" shouted Colin. They bolted.

"Stay together! Stay together!" Shawn choked as he ran.

But it was impossible.

Shawn's eyes blurred, filled with tears from the stinging smoke. He lunged blindly through the trees, following the noise of the others crashing through the brush. The heat was horrible. Sparks sizzled through the air. Out of the corner of his streaming eyes, Shawn thought he glimpsed a large, dark shape racing through the trees just off to his left. Was it an animal or a person? He couldn't be sure.

"Petra! Craig!" he gasped. "Where are you? Tony!"

He thought he heard Craig shout in reply and swerved towards the sound. His brother's panicked face loomed out of the smoke. Shawn grabbed Craig's sleeve and towed him forward.

"Come on! Come on!"

Another figure materialized out of the smoky gloom, loping along beside them. Colin. The boys couldn't spare any breath for talk. They needed every molecule of oxygen they could suck out of this toxic air just to keep moving.

They ran until every breath felt like a knife sliding in and out of their lungs.

Finally the roar of the fire receded. The smoke thinned slightly. Abruptly, the forest ended, spitting them out into a bowl-shaped valley, hemmed in on three sides by cliffs of white gypsum. The boys staggered to a halt.

Still coughing and gagging from the smoke, Shawn looked around him.

"Where are the others?"

"Don't know," wheezed Colin. He was bent over, panting, his hands on his knees. "Lost sight of them in the smoke."

Craig ran back to the entrance of the valley and cupped his hands around his mouth.

"Tony! Petra!" he called.

Shawn joined him, shouting at the indifferent trees.

"Petra! Tony! Hobart!" But his voice, ragged from exhaustion and smoke, couldn't penetrate the smoky forest. There was no answer.

The Bullroarer

Shawn looked around desperately.

Before him lay the forest and the approaching fire. Behind him were rugged white cliffs of crumbling gypsum. Beneath his feet, a carpet of tinder-dry grass rustled beneath his sneakers.

"What do we do now?" asked Craig, looking up at his big brother, his blue eyes wide and frightened. Shawn glanced over at Colin, but the older boy was also looking at him expectantly, waiting for an answer. Shawn squared his shoulders and took a deep breath.

"We stick to the plan. We head for the White Caves and take shelter underground." Shawn dug into his pocket and handed the pin to Colin. "Find some water and take another bearing," Shawn ordered. "Make sure we know where north is." Colin nodded and sprinted towards the cliffs at the back of the valley. Shawn began criss-crossing the clearing, scouring the ground. Craig bounced along beside him, peppering him with anxious questions.

"How are we going to get out of here, Shawn? What do we do when the fire reaches the valley? What about Tony and Petra? How are we going to find them?"

"We're going to call them."

"Call them? With what? We don't have a phone."

"I'm going to make something."

"You're going to make a *phone*?"

Shawn stopped and knelt. He brushed aside the tall, swaying grasses to reveal a shallow stream. It cut a narrow, curving course across the valley floor. Shawn stood up, cupped his hands around his mouth, and called to Colin: "Hey! I found water!"

From the back cliff wall, Colin gave them the thumbs-up. "I know—it's coming from over here!" his thin voice came back. "There's a spring coming up from beneath the cliff!"

"Go ahead and drink," Shawn told Craig. "Spring water is naturally filtered by the earth. This is probably better than the bottled stuff Mom buys at the store." Both brothers scooped frantic handfuls of the icy-fresh water into their mouths before splashing it over their sooty, sweaty faces. Shawn shook the water out of his eyes. He stood up and squinted again at the small figure of Colin over by the far cliff. He was drinking, too.

"Colin! Did you take a bearing?" called Shawn. "Which way is north?"

Colin turned and pointed directly at the sheer rock face behind him.

"Great," muttered Shawn. Craig tugged at his brother's sleeve impatiently. "Shawn! How are we going to make a phone?"

"We're not going to make a phone."

"Then how are you going to call Petra and Tony?"

But Shawn was busy running his hands along the stream bed. In a few minutes, he found what he was looking for: a narrow strip of deadwood, worn smooth by the endless rippling of the water. Shawn fished out the thin, ruler-sized piece of wood and ran back towards the narrow mouth of the valley. Smoke was wafting from between the trees, slowly filling the valley. Colin jogged over to them.

"What's with the wood?" he asked.

"Shawn's building a phone," Craig told him.

"Huh?"

"Craig, I need your twine," said Shawn.

Craig pulled his string collection out of his pocket and handed it to Shawn. Shawn unravelled it. He looked up. "We need to make a small hole in the end of the wood so we can attach the string. Anybody got anything sharp?"

Colin pulled out a small red jackknife. It had multiple blades that folded out.

"Oh, cool!" breathed Craig. "I wish I was allowed to have one of those!"

"It's a real Swiss Army knife," Colin said proudly. "My dad sent it from overseas. The corkscrew might work." A few seconds and some sawdust later, the hole was made. Shawn fed the end of the twine through the hole and tied it off.

Playing out about four feet of string, Shawn stood

up and dangled the piece of wood until it hung just above the ground.

"Give it a spin for me," he instructed Colin. "We need to twist the string. Hurry!"

Colin flicked the piece of wood, sending it spinning in place at the end of the string.

"Okay. Give me some room," said Shawn. Colin and Craig moved several paces back. In the centre of the clearing, Shawn began to swing the rope around his head like a lasso. Around and around it went. The piece of wood sliced through the air in a swooping arc. A strange, unearthly moaning filled the clearing.

Craig clapped his hands over his ears. "Whoa— what *is* that thing?"

"It's called a bullroarer!" Shawn yelled over the noise. "Aboriginal people around the world used to use these to send messages over long distances."

The strange buzzing wail filled the clearing.

"Some people believed that the sound of the bullroarer was the spirit-voices of their dead ancestors," Shawn said.

"It does sound freaky," said Colin. "Kind of like a ghost."

"Like a ghost imitating a chainsaw, maybe!" said Craig, his hands still over his ears.

"It's all about frequency and vibration," said Shawn, "with a little aerodynamics thrown in. We can change the pitch and frequency by slowing the movement…"

Letting out more string, he swung the bullroarer in a bigger, slower circle. The sound dropped to a deep, vibrating moan.

"Lower sound frequencies travel farther," said Shawn as he continued to swing the bullroarer. "Hopefully Tony and Petra will hear the noise and follow it."

"Unless Tony thinks it's a ghost," said Craig. "Then he might run the opposite way!"

In the smoky gloom of the valley, the bullroarer moaned and wailed.

"This is creeping me out," said Colin.

"It's a good way to attract attention," said Shawn determinedly, still swinging the strange instrument.

And then—

"Look!" yelped Craig.

"Something's coming out of the bushes!" Colin yelled at the same time.

The branches parted and two sooty, dirty figures half-stumbled, half-fell into the clearing.

"Tony!" cried Craig.

"Petra!" shouted Shawn. He dropped the bullroarer and ran towards his fallen friends.

Colin got there first.

The teenager scooped the half-conscious girl into his arms and ran towards the cliff. "They need water!" he called over his shoulder. Craig and Shawn hoisted Tony to his feet. Draping his arms around their shoulders, they towed Tony towards the cliff wall.

Head lolling, Tony still managed to roll a pair of incredulous eyes at Shawn.

"What the HECK was making that freakishly weird sound, man?" he gasped through parched lips. "I thought for sure Petra was leading us straight to the Gates of Ghostville."

Craig patted his friend's arm soothingly. "No ghosts, Tony. We didn't have a phone so Shawn made a bullroarer instead."

Tony blinked at him through bleary, red-rimmed eyes. "Oh. Well, that makes perfect sense."

At the base of the cliff, Colin was easing Petra next to the spring that burbled up from beneath the rocks. Gently, he dribbled some water onto her cracked, dry lips. Petra groaned and coughed. She opened her eyes. Looked into his dark ones.

"Colin," she whispered. Surprise and gratitude flickered through the exhaustion in her face. "You saved us!"

Colin opened his mouth, but before he could speak, there was a thud, and then a yelp from Tony as he landed in a heap on the ground beside them.

"Ow! Geez, Shawn! Warn me the next time you're about to drop me, will ya? I appreciate the lift, man, but your landing could use a little work!"

Tony's complaints went unheeded. Shawn had already turned on his heel and was striding away across the clearing.

"What's up with him?" Tony asked.

Shawn picked up the bullroarer from where it had landed in the grass. He turned it over. To his surprise, his hands were shaking.

Well, why shouldn't they be shaking after all we've been through today? Shawn thought angrily. He squeezed the bullroarer to stop the trembling in his hands. He felt the sharp edges of the wood digging into his palms. He squeezed harder and took a deep breath. That was shaky, too.

What do I care if Petra thinks Colin saved her? Shawn thought. What did it matter, anyway? Sure, maybe Colin had warned them about the Pits of Despair. And maybe he had told them about the White Caves...but they weren't exactly *saved* yet, were they? And it wasn't *Colin's* bullroarer that had called Petra and Tony out of the burning forest.

Shawn felt a splinter drive deep into the heel of his hand. He loosened his grip on the bullroarer and began wrapping the string around it with tight, angry jerks. Well, Petra could think what she liked about Colin, Shawn decided, shoving the bullroarer into his back pocket. If that scrawny, shaggy-haired teen was her idea of a hero, that was just fine with him...

A loud cracking sound interrupted Shawn's moody thoughts. His head snapped up in time to see a hoary old poplar tree, its head wreathed in flames, tipping forward in slow motion. As Shawn watched, transfixed, the tree fell across the mouth of the valley, slamming into the ground in a shower of sparks.

For a long second, the tree lay in silence, like a fallen soldier.

Then, a tiny flame crawled out from beneath the body of the dead tree and began licking the dry grass at the edge of the clearing. Another followed. And then another. The flames grew and multiplied, devouring the valley floor with ravenous intensity.

"Uh, guys?" called Shawn, backing away from the advancing army of hungry flames. "We need to find a way out of here—RIGHT NOW!"

Climb for Your Life!

"Hurry, Shawn!"

Craig was waving frantically at his brother from across the valley. He and the others had already scrambled on top of a pile of boulders heaped at the bottom of the cliff. Shawn sprinted across the clearing towards them. Behind him, he could hear the snickering of the flames as they chewed their way through the dry grass.

When he reached the clutter of rocks, Petra stretched out her hand. Taking it, Shawn swung himself up onto the boulder beside her. "Glad you could make it," she said, with a tense smile.

"Oh, you know me," panted Shawn. "I wouldn't miss a good time like this."

"But are you up for that?" asked Tony, jerking his thumb at the cliff rising above them.

"There's a path," said Craig, pulling at Shawn's sleeve and pointing. "There. See?"

Shawn ran his eyes over the rugged rock wall and finally spotted what Craig was optimistically calling a path. A narrow ledge of crumbling rock ran diagonally up the rock on a sharp incline.

"It's, um, pretty narrow," said Shawn.

"It's wide enough for a sneaker," argued Craig. "In most places."

"We should have rock-climbing gear, man," said Tony, shaking his head. "You know, ropes and helmets and stuff. We'd be crazy to tackle a climb like that without proper equipment!"

"We'll be dead if we don't," said Shawn grimly. It was true. The fire was mowing its way across the grass towards them. Soon, very soon, this stone-walled valley would be a cauldron of fire. And the only way out was *up*.

Pressing themselves flat against the cliff face, the five young people inched their way along the treacherous path. Rocks rolled away beneath their sneakers and went rattling and bouncing down into the valley below. Shawn was leading. Craig had argued, saying that since *he* saw the path, *he* should be the one to go first. But Shawn had vetoed this, pointing out that his longer arms and legs made it easier for him to feel out the safest route, checking for the best handholds and footholds. A brief headlock convinced Craig that Shawn was right, and he followed behind his big brother with only a minimal amount of grumbling. Petra came after Craig, with Colin behind her. Tony brought up the rear.

The smoke wound itself around their necks and limbs as if it was trying to pluck them off the cliff. Shawn blinked his stinging eyes and reached for a tree root protruding from a crevice. He gave it a cautious tug. It held. He gripped it firmly, and pulled himself across yet another gap in the ledge.

"There's a break in the path there," he called back to the others. "Use the tree root to help you get across."

Craig swung himself quickly across the gap, and edged along the ledge to where Shawn was waiting. Petra came next. She grabbed the tree root, but just as she shifted her weight to step over the gap, the tree root came loose, slithering out of the crevice like a snake. Petra flailed backwards over the yawning valley with a small, strangled shriek.

"Petra!" cried Shawn. He lunged back towards her, knowing that she was impossibly out of reach. A hand snapped out and grabbed Petra's arm, pulling her back against the cliff face.

"You okay?" asked Colin.

"Sure," gasped Petra. She gave him a shaky smile. "Thanks, Colin. You saved me again. It's a good thing you're here."

Shawn gritted his teeth and looked away.

"Don't worry about it, bro," Craig told him in a low voice. "You couldn't know that the root would let go."

Shawn shook his head without looking at his brother. He didn't trust himself to speak. It was his fault that Petra had almost fallen off the cliff. He should have tested that tree root more carefully. He was leading. He couldn't afford to make mistakes.

One misstep, one wrong decision, might cost his best friends their lives. He suddenly felt sick to his stomach. Shawn closed his eyes and pressed his sweaty forehead against the cool rock of the cliff.

"Hey, kid—you all right?" It was Colin's voice. "You want me to take over? I could lead for a while."

Shawn shook his head fiercely. "I'm fine." He forced himself to look at the precarious route ahead.

"Shawn?" Behind him, Petra's voice was anxious.

"It's okay," he croaked. "Follow me. We're almost there."

"Shawn, buddy—I don't want to rush you or anything," called Tony from the back of the line, "but we should probably pick up the pace, or that fire's going to beat us to the top of the cliff!"

Shawn looked around and realized with a sinking feeling that Tony was right. The fire had spread out from the mouth of the valley in both directions, following the treeline up the steep, rocky ridge and onto the clifftops encircling the valley. Soon the two lines of fire would meet, closing the circle at the top of the back cliff wall that they were now scaling.

"Climb!" cried Shawn. "Everybody, climb for your life!"

They did.

There didn't waste breath on talking. They climbed as fast as they dared, grabbing at rocks and roots, ignoring scraped knuckles and knees, hugging the white wall of the cliff. Small rivers of dirt and gravel, knocked loose by their scrabbling feet, showered down into the valley below.

"Almost there," grunted Shawn.

The top of the cliff jutted out in a pouting lip. It was a hairy lip, too—shaggy with fine, spidery tree roots and lichen that dangled beneath the earthy outcropping like a crazy moustache. Shawn pulled himself up beneath the overhang. To reach the top, he would have to swing himself out, away from the cliff, then up and over the underside of the ledge.

Craig eyed Shawn's chosen route nervously.

"How are you going to get up there, Shawn?"

"I'll manage. You wait there until I can help you up."

"Shawn," called Petra worriedly, "I think we should try to get up someplace else."

"We don't have time," Shawn said. "Once I'm up, I'll be able to pull you guys over the top."

"Be careful, kid," said Colin.

"Good luck, pal," gulped Tony. "Try to think like Spider-Man!"

Shawn reached up and grabbed two fistfuls of the tree roots hanging down around his ears from the roof of the overhang. Wrapping them once tightly around his hands, he yanked hard. The roots held firm. Gripping the roots, Shawn pulled his knees in to his chest and kicked his feet up hard, so that they were braced on the underside of the ledge.

"Just like the rings in gymnastics," he grunted.

"Way to go, Spidey!" cheered Tony from somewhere below.

Shawn inched forward. He felt like a beetle crawling along the ceiling. At the edge of the overhang, he threw his right arm up and over the top ledge, his fingers scrambling to find something, anything, that would bear his weight. He knocked a rock loose. It fell past his head and went bouncing down the cliff.

Shawn felt around blindly. Aha! An old tree root, thick and gnarly, met his exploring fingers. The root was pressed tight into the earth. Shawn scraped at the dirt with his fingernails until he could worm his whole hand underneath the root. It pinched his hand against the ground, but at least he would be unlikely to lose his grip.

Under the overhang, Shawn was now forced to let go of the tree-root moustache with his left hand. He flung his left arm out and up as fast as he could, trying to get two hands on the gnarled root above him before gravity kicked in.

An impossible move.

With no way to brace his feet, Shawn fell, dangling by one arm as his body went swinging out over the valley like a pendulum.

Dimly, Shawn heard the cries and shouts of his friends, but the sound seemed to come from a great distance. Pain shot up his arm. His hand was pinned under the tree root like a vice, while his body hung from it, twisting helplessly in space. He could feel his shoulder starting to part from its socket.

His brain clouded over with pain and terror. *It was hopeless from the beginning*, he now realized. *Nobody could survive this. We're all going to—*

"SHAWN!" Colin's voice roared, cutting through his panicked thoughts. "Are you going to hang around like a Christmas ornament all day or do you want me to come up there and hold your hand? GET UP ON THAT LEDGE *RIGHT NOW!*"

Anger jolted through Shawn like an electric shock. He kicked his legs furiously and managed to touch the cliff wall with the tips of his sneakers. It was all he needed. Pushing off with his toes, Shawn launched himself upward. His fingernails caught the edge of the ledge. Every muscle in his body was screaming as he hauled himself up, inch by painful inch, and then suddenly—he was over the top! He lay still for a moment, trying to breathe through the red-hot pain in his shoulder and hand.

"Shawn?" Petra called. "Are you okay?"

Shawn started to get up, and then fell back—he was still anchored to the ground by the tree root. Gingerly, he worked his fingers loose and pulled his hand free of the root's life-saving grip. His fingers were a rosy purple. There was a black bruise running across his palm, and his knuckles were starting to swell to an impressive size. Wincing, he wiggled his fingers carefully. They hurt, but at least he could move them.

"Shawn?" It was Craig's voice now.

Shawn poked his head over the cliff and looked down. Dizziness washed over him as he realized just how high they had climbed. His friends and his little brother still clung to the wall like ants.

"I'm okay," he said, stretching his good arm down over the ledge towards them. "Come on up and take my hand. I'll pull you over the tricky bit."

Race for the White Caves

"Wow. That was extreme," wheezed Tony.

They were all sprawled, panting, on the clifftop. Once Shawn had hauled Craig over the ledge, the two brothers had worked together to pull the other three to safety.

"We should get extra phys. ed. credit for that," added Tony. Below them, the valley was engulfed in flames.

There was no time to rest. On either side, lines of fire were closing in on them. The five young people staggered to their feet and sprinted through the smoke-filled forest. Spot fires were now springing up all around them, spawned by the countless sparks that swirled like sinister seed pods through the toxic air.

A trail appeared in front of them. As one, they swung onto it. Then Colin yelled and pointed to a piece of red-painted tin nailed to a crooked pine tree.

"It's a trail marker! I recognize this spot! I know where we are," Colin said excitedly as he ran to the tree. "The White Caves should be just on the other side of that gully!" Colin pointed across a tree-filled ravine to their right.

At that second, there was a loud *WHOOSH!*

Behind them, an expansive beech tree exploded into

flames. Immediately, the trees on either side of the great beech ignited into twin fireballs. Like mutating meteors, the fireballs leapt from treetop to treetop.

"Crown fire!" yelled Petra, staring in horror at the approaching inferno.

"*RUN*!" shouted all the kids together. They dove into the ravine, skidding and sliding on its shifting carpet of dead leaves and pine needles.

"We're never going to reach the caves in time," moaned Petra.

"There must be something we can do!" panted Shawn as he vaulted over a dead log. "What does your Uncle Daryl say? How do you survive a forest fire?"

"You don't," Petra answered through clenched teeth. "You *avoid* a forest fire…you don't *survive* it."

Petra shook her head as she stumbled after him. "We tried, Shawn. We tried harder than anything. *You* tried harder than anything, but…" A single tear slid down her sooty cheek. "Nobody can outrun a fire like this. Nobody can survive—that." She gestured hopelessly at the approaching firestorm. She smiled sideways at him and gave a sad little shrug of her shoulder. "It's game over. I guess you can't win 'em all."

Shawn's throat tightened painfully. In spite of the danger, he stopped short and spun Petra around to face him. His serious grey eyes held her frightened green ones. "Listen," he said. "Maybe we can't win them all, but we're going to win *this* one. Do you hear me? Because there is no way I am losing you or Craig or

Tony or even..." Shawn winced just a little. "Or even Colin, today. Understand?"

"What about Hobie?" said Petra in a choked voice.

"He'll turn up," said Shawn. "I know he will."

"Guys!" Tony was galloping back towards them. "What are you doing just standing around? This is no time to hold a committee meeting!" They turned with him and fled up the other side of the ravine.

"Come on, come on!" urged Colin and Craig from the top of the slope. In a moment, Shawn, Petra, and Tony had reached them, and the five were scrambling along the narrow, rocky footpath that dipped and twisted along the top of the ravine.

Soot and ash were swirling everywhere. Glowing embers whizzed past them like white-hot shrapnel.

It was unbearably hot.

"Now I know how a chocolate-chip cookie feels when you put it in the oven!" gasped Tony.

"How far now?" gasped Shawn.

"Almost there!" wheezed Colin. "Keep going!"

"Wait!" Tony suddenly called over the roar of the fire. "What's that noise?"

"That's the sound of the forest exploding," Petra told him. "Now, *come on*!"

"No!" Tony insisted. "That *other* noise!"

Over the din of the crackling flames, a droning whine could just be heard. And it was getting louder.

"I know that sound!" said Tony. "That's a—a—"

"Plane!" yelled Craig.

The Scooper

The drone of the plane's engine grew louder.

"Where is it? Do you see it?" cried Tony, craning his neck to see through the branches and the roiling smoke.

"There it is!" cried Petra.

"Where? *Where*?"

"There!" She pointed. High above the branches, the yellow belly of an aircraft could just be glimpsed, scudding in and out between the heavy clouds of smoke.

Tony started doing jumping jacks, waving his arms crazily. "We're here! We're down here! Hey! Search-and-rescue guys! We're over here!" he hollered at the top of his voice. Shawn grabbed Tony's arm, pulling his bouncing friend back to earth.

"They can't hear you, Tony. They can't even see us under all this brush."

"Uh, guys?" said Craig, peering hard at the plane.

"Quick!" Tony said frantically. "We have to signal them and let them know where we are!"

"Guys—" said Craig, a little louder.

"I know!" said Tony, feverishly snatching up some

branches from the side of the trail. "We can build a torch!"

The others stared at him.

Tony looked from the little sticks clutched in his hand to the towering trunks of flaming trees. He dropped the sticks. "Okay. Maybe a torch isn't the best way to get their attention right now."

"GUYS!" yelled Craig.

The others spun around in surprise.

"That is NOT a search-and-rescue plane," said Craig.

"How do *you* know?" retorted Tony.

"Trust me, he knows," said Shawn. "Craig's a walking encyclopedia of airplane facts ever since we went up in that helicopter last winter."

"Who cares what kind of plane it is as long as it rescues us?" said Tony. He turned and waved his arms at the sky. "Yoo-hoo, whatever-kind-of-plane-you-are! Come and get us!"

"Tony!" said Craig again, clutching at his arm. "We have to get out of here!"

"Well, *duh*," said Tony crossly. "Why do you think I'm trying to flag down a plane?"

Craig threw another wide-eyed look at the oncoming aircraft. "No, Tony, you don't understand. That's a Canadair CL-215!"

Tony looked at Shawn. "What'd he say?"

Shawn shook his head. "No idea."

"A Scooper!" spluttered Craig. "It's a Scooper!"

"Is he speaking English?" Tony wanted to know, as Craig hopped up and down with impatience, trying to pull them off the trail.

"Craig," Petra said, putting a hand on his arm. "Calm down. What's a Scooper?"

"A water bomber," gasped Craig. "That's a water bomber coming towards us!"

"Well, that's the best news I've heard all day!" said Tony, a relieved grin spreading across his face. "We get saved from a fiery death *and* get a cool, refreshing shower all at once. Excellent!"

Craig groaned. "Tony! Do you know how much water the Canadair CL-215 carries?"

"I'm sure you're going to tell me," said Tony.

"It can scoop up over five thousand litres of water from a lake in a single pass in just ten seconds. *That's* why they call it the Scooper."

"Cool!" said Tony. "This is going to be just like Splash Mountain!" He opened his arms wide, lifted his face skyward, and closed his eyes. "I'm ready!" he called. "Drench me!"

"TONY!" said Craig.

"*What?*" said Tony.

"Do you even know how much five thousand litres of water weighs?"

"Um…" said Tony.

"Ten thousand pounds," said Craig.

"That's, um, about five tons," said Petra, calculating. Her eyes widened. "Uh-oh."

The drone of the approaching plane became a roar.

"Did you say five tons?" Tony gulped.

The hulking yellow body of the Scooper burst out of the swirling clouds and smoke.

"Run!" yelled Shawn.

They whirled and bolted through the trees.

"Go away!" yelled Tony, flapping his hands at the oncoming plane as if it were an angry hornet. "Shoo! Get back! There are kids down here, you know!"

But the plane continued barrelling along its flight path, oblivious to their presence. It zoomed towards them, dropping lower and lower. The noise of its engines rose to a deafening thunder.

"This way!" shouted Colin, scrambling up a lumpy hill full of moss-covered boulders.

There was a roar.

But it wasn't from the plane's engines.

This was a different sort of roar.

A Niagara Falls sort of roar.

An avalanche of white water—nearly five tons of it—crashed down into the gully, just to the side of them.

Tree trunks snapped like toothpicks and were swept down into the ravine in a landslide of mud, boulders, and water. A cloud of white vapour hissed angrily into the air.

"Whoaaaa!!" yelled the kids, gaping at the huge, muddy trench that the water had gouged out of the hillside.

"Holy cranky catfish, that was close!" gasped Tony.

"Look out—here comes another one!" yelled Craig. Sure enough, the whine of another Scooper could be heard above the treetops.

"Oh, man!" moaned Tony.

"Follow me!" yelled Colin. He scrambled the rest of the way up the rocky hill…and disappeared from sight.

"Where'd he go?" Shawn yelled. He glanced around wildly. The fire was advancing on all sides now. A few metres away, a fir tree burst into flame. "Come on!" Motioning the others to follow, Shawn clambered up to the peak where Colin had vanished. And stopped short.

A sinkhole, bigger than any other they'd seen, gaped at their feet. At the bottom of the pit, white boulders reared up like teeth from some giant, prehistoric beast…and behind them yawned the black mouth of a cave.

"Oh man," breathed Tony.

Just then, with a noise like a hundred hungry chainsaws, the Scooper punched through the smoke like a great, yellow bird of prey. It rumbled towards them, dropping lower…lower. There was a mechanical whine as the cargo doors in its huge belly started to open…

"*Jump!*" yelled Shawn.

The White Cave

Shawn launched himself into the air above the sinkhole. The white jaws of the cave gaped wide as its black throat rushed up to swallow him. At the same instant, there was a horrific roar. The world flashed from white to black, and the air suddenly became liquid. Freezing water enveloped him. Shawn felt himself tumbling over and over. It was like being inside a washing machine. Hard objects pummelled his body, sending him crashing against even harder objects. He had no idea which way was up and which way was down. He was drowning in a deafening darkness.

Then rock was pressing against him, squeezing him on all sides.

And still the water sucked at him, pulling his body along an impossibly tight channel. It was heart-stoppingly cold. Shawn tried to lift his face above the water, but his head smacked against solid stone.

I'm going to drown, he thought in disbelief. *I lived through a forest fire only to drown underground!*

And suddenly he was angry. Furious.

No way! Shawn thought. *Not like this. Not after coming this far...*

He thrashed his legs wildly, clawing at the rock with his fingers, propelling himself forward. His lungs were bursting. A red haze swam in front of his eyes.

He had to breathe. He *had* to.

His fingernails scraped desperately against the rock. His kicks became weaker.

In another second it would be over. Shawn knew what would happen.

He would open his mouth and his aching lungs would expand one last time, sucking in the freezing water. And its liquid blackness would fill him, turning him into nothingness from the inside out.

Suddenly the rock walls fell away from his scrabbling fingers. The tunnel abruptly released its vice-like grip on his body, ejecting him into a dark, subterranean void in a primal gush of water.

And then the water was gone.

It dropped him like a broken toy and retreated, muttering and hissing, into invisible cracks and crevices. Shawn was left sprawling on a slab of wet rock. Coughing and choking, he retched up a bellyful of water. For a long time he lay there, gulping air into his waterlogged body and trying to remember how to move. Finally he was able to roll over and push himself into a sitting position.

It was absolutely black.

Shawn raised his hand in front of his face. He couldn't see it. He moved his hand closer. It was freaky—he knew his hand was there, but it was utterly invisible. He waited for his eyes to adjust to the darkness.

They didn't.

Shawn moved his hand closer until he felt his palm brush the tip of his nose. He still couldn't make out even the faintest outline of his hand. The darkness was absolute.

"Craig?" he choked out.

His voice had a hollow, echoing sound.

"Petra? Tony? *Anyone*?"

Trapped

"Ohhhhh," groaned Tony. "That wasn't *nearly* as fun as Splash Mountain!"

He picked himself up from the wet floor of the cave, rubbing his backside.

"No kidding," moaned Petra. She moved out of the shadows into the dim, watery light that seemed to be leaking from behind a mess of rubble somewhere above her head. "I feel like a goldfish that just got flushed down the toilet. Are you okay, Craig?"

There was a rattle of loose rock and then a splash as Craig slid down from on top of a boulder and dropped into the puddle beside them.

"I'm okay," he said. "Soggy, and a little banged up, but still in one piece. How about you, Shawn?"

No answer.

"Shawn?"

They peered into the recesses of the cave, waiting for one of the shadows to shift and morph into a slim, sandy-haired boy. But no figure emerged from the darkness.

"Oh, no…" whispered Petra.

"Shawn!" Craig called again, in alarm. His voice echoed weirdly off of the stone walls.

A tall, slim figure staggered out from behind a column of rock.

"*There* you are!" Petra exclaimed in relief, sloshing through the water towards him. "Are you all right, Shawn?"

The tall boy shook his head and limped towards them.

"What's wrong? Are you hurt?" Petra asked, concern sharpening her voice.

The boy shook his head again. "There's nothing wrong with me...except that I'm not Shawn," the figure answered in a wry voice. He moved into the feeble light.

It was Colin.

"Sorry to disappoint you," he said.

"Oh!" Petra started in surprise. "Colin! I'm not dis—I mean, I thought you were—I'm glad you're safe," she said awkwardly. "You're limping," she added.

Colin grimaced. "Twisted my ankle when I jumped. No biggie. We're missing somebody?"

"Shawn," Craig told him, worried. "We can't find him."

"Did he make it into the cave?" Colin asked.

"I—I'm not sure..." said Petra uneasily. "We all jumped and, well, everything's kind of a blur after that."

But Colin was already climbing up a scree-littered slope towards the source of the light.

"Hey—where are you going?" Petra demanded.

"The cave entrance is up here," said Colin shortly. "Maybe Shawn is, too."

Colin's head and shoulders disappeared behind a great, lopsided boulder perched at the top of the rocky incline. They heard him scrabbling among the rocks. Some loose stones and a few twigs and branches slithered down past his feet and fell to the cave floor in front of them. They heard Colin swearing softly under his breath.

"What's up?" Tony called. There was no answer. Up in the shadows, Colin was grunting and huffing like he was struggling to lift something very heavy.

"Hey! Pyro Boy! What's the deal?" Tony called in a louder voice.

With an angry grunt, Colin scuttled backwards and dropped back down beside them.

"The *deal* is that the cave entrance is blocked with trees and rocks and mud washed down by the water bomber. We're sealed in. And don't call me Pyro Boy!"

"Any sign of Shawn?" Craig asked. Colin shook his head. Craig swallowed hard. Colin patted the younger boy's shoulder awkwardly. "Don't worry, kid. Your brother's probably on the other side of that mess trying to dig us out right now."

"Yeah, you're probably right," said Craig,

brightening. But Colin's dark eyes met Petra's worried ones and the thought passed unspoken between them: *Or maybe he's under that mess, buried in mangled trees and mud.*

"So, Pyro Boy, what's your plan for getting out of here, seeing as the White Caves were *your* brilliant idea and all?" said Tony.

"You're alive, aren't you?" growled Colin. "And I said, DON'T call me Pyro Boy!"

"Oh, I'm sorry," said Tony with exaggerated politeness. "Would you rather be known as the Human Torch instead?"

With a cry, Colin launched himself at Tony in a flying tackle. Both boys went down in a pile of flailing fists and kicking feet.

"Oh, for Pete's sake," groaned Petra.

"Guys, guys—break it up!" pleaded Craig, hovering over the scuffling pair.

Petra bent down over the puddle of water on the cave floor. Using her hands as a scoop, she sloshed the icy-cold water over the two fighting boys: "KNOCK. IT. *OFF!*" she ordered.

Spluttering, the two boys rolled apart, glaring at each other.

"I did *not* start that fire!" Colin insisted in a ragged voice. "And just so you know, I've been watching that fawn ever since it was born in the spring. I never, *ever* meant for those guys to chase it. I never meant for any of this—" he broke off, his voice thick with misery. Stumbling to his feet, Colin limped away into the shadows at the back of the cave.

"Geez, Tony," muttered Petra, giving him a shove.

"What? What did I say?" asked Tony.

Petra sighed. "You guys check out the cave mouth. See if you can pull away any of the debris and at least see through to the outside. We need to know if the fire's out…and maybe Shawn is out there." Petra tried to sound hopeful, for Craig's sake.

"What are *you* going to do?" Craig wanted to know.

"I'm going to talk to Colin."

Petra picked her way carefully across the uneven, rocky floor. A shallow stream chuckled its way through the centre of the cavern before disappearing into the blackness at the back of the cave. Petra hopped over the water and felt her way along the cave wall. It was very dark. She almost bumped into Colin before she saw him. He was sitting slumped against a boulder, his head in his hands.

"Hey," said Petra.

"What do you want?" mumbled Colin.

"You okay?"

"Swell," muttered Colin. He shook his head and rubbed his sleeve roughly over his eyes. Sighing heavily, he turned to face Petra.

"Look," he said. "I'm sorry you guys had to get stuck with me. I know you all hate me and I don't blame you, so just pretend like I'm not here, okay?"

Petra looked into the dark, pain-filled eyes of the

older boy. She regarded him in silence for a moment.

"I don't hate you," she said at last. "I mean, I did when I saw you in the quarry, but I don't now. I think you were in the wrong place at the wrong time with the wrong guys."

"No kidding," said Colin. "I was stupid—so *stupid*—to bring them there!" He slapped his hand against the cave wall in frustration.

"I won't argue with you on that one," said Petra. "It was dumb. And you went along with what those jerks were doing, which was way dumber."

"Thanks for pointing that out," said Colin. A shudder shook his body and he covered his face with his hands. "This is so messed up! The forest, all those animals…So much is gone. How am I ever going to fix this? How can I ever make this right?"

Petra hesitated, then reached out a hand and touched Colin's shoulder.

"Some things can't be fixed," she said quietly. "Sometimes all we can do is to try to make things better than they are."

Colin raised his head and looked at her. His cheeks were wet.

"I don't know what to do," he said, simply.

"You're already doing it," Petra said. "You're helping us. You helped us get through the Pits of Despair. You carried me away from the fire and across that valley. You helped Shawn on the cliff by making him mad enough to fight his way to the top."

Colin looked up at her in surprise.

Petra shrugged. "*I* knew what you were doing back there, even if Shawn didn't. *And*," she continued, "you brought us to the White Caves. We made it through fire *and* water because of you." She punched him lightly on the arm. "So you see? You're already doing something. A lot, actually."

"But is it enough?" asked Colin.

"It's enough for right now," Petra said, turning back in the direction of the others. "And we still need your help. This isn't over yet."

"I'm not sure the others see it that way."

"They will."

"Not Tony."

"Yeah, well, you have to excuse Tony," Petra said, as she headed back towards the cave mouth. "He suffers from verbal diarrhea. You can safely ignore at least fifty percent of whatever he says."

"I heard that!" Tony's indignant voice came from the darkness just ahead of them. His round face and bristly hair materialized out of the shadows. "And I'll have you know that *some* people actually *appreciate* my gift of gab, my charming chatter, my vibrant verbiage…"

"You see what I mean?" said Petra, rolling her eyes at Colin.

"…my eloquent locution, my proclivity for loquaciousness, my oral artistry…"

"Tony!" snapped Petra, interrupting him.

"What?"

"Did you have something to tell us?"

"Huh? Oh, yeah…Craig and I checked out the cave mouth and Pyro—I mean, Colin—is right. It's totally blocked."

"Do you have any *good* news?"

"Well, there are a few gaps that we can see through—"

"Which would explain the little bit of light we have down here," put in Colin.

"—and it looks like the water bomber put out the worst of the flames, from what we can see of the sinkhole, anyway."

"Any sign of Shawn?" asked Petra, her voice tightening.

Tony shook his head. "No…nothing."

"Which means," said Petra, "that either he's not outside the cave, or…" She stopped, swallowing hard.

"Or he's in no shape to answer," Tony finished grimly.

"There's another possibility," said Colin.

"What?" asked Petra and Tony.

"That he's here inside the cave."

"Where?" demanded Petra, spreading her arms wide. "There's just this one cavern. We're here and he's not. Where else could he be?"

Holes in the Dark

"The water found a way out of this cavern," Colin said as he started running his hands along the cave wall. "Maybe we can find one, too."

"You think Shawn got swept away with the water?" asked Petra.

"Maybe."

There were footsteps and then Craig was at Petra's shoulder.

"What's keeping you guys?" he asked anxiously. "Did you find something?"

"Not yet," Colin told him. "Caves don't give up their secrets easily. Everybody, spread out," he ordered. "Feel around with your hands. Check the walls for any holes, crevices, or cracks."

They did, sloshing back and forth across the icy stream that trickled through the heart of the cave. Fanning out to different sections of the cave, the kids ran their hands over the cold, damp walls. Craig slipped on what looked like a shiny rock.

"Whoa!" he exclaimed. "Holy crow—there's ice down here!"

Colin nodded. "There's ice in these caves even in the

middle of summer," he said. "It never gets warmer than two or three degrees down here."

"Ice," moaned Tony. "Why did it have to be ice? I *hate* ice!" He shivered and rubbed his arms. "Brrrr, it's cold! What I would give for a nice, warm fire!"

The others stared at him.

"What?" said Tony, holding up his hands. "I meant a *little* fire. Geez."

"Actually, Tony's right," said Petra. "It *is* really cold, and all of us are wet. If we don't get out of here soon, hypothermia is a very real possibility…as much as I hate to say it."

"Oh, man," groaned Tony. "Out of the fire and into the freezer! And did you *have* to say the H-word?"

"Hey, guys—I found something!" Craig had crawled up a sloping section of rock and was prying into the dark space where the cave roof met the wall. "There's an opening up here!"

"I've got news for you," came Colin's voice from the far back corner of the cave. "There's an opening down here, too!"

The kids scrambled to look in first one and then the other of the openings. Both were small, dark, and forbidding looking. They returned to the centre of the cave and huddled together in the chilly darkness.

"So what do we do now?" said Craig.

"Well, we've got two choices," said Petra, nodding in the direction of the two small holes that the boys had discovered. "Do we take the high road or the low road?"

"We could split up," said Craig.

"No way," said Tony. "Don't you ever watch TV? Splitting up is never a good idea. Somebody always ends up getting ambushed by aliens or murdered by mummies or swallowed by snakes or tortured by tarantulas or—"

"TONY!" snapped Petra.

"What?"

"We get the picture."

"Oh. Okay."

There was a pause. The only sound was the *drip-drip-drip* of water in the cold, clammy darkness.

"M-m-maybe we should stick together…" suggested Craig in a small voice.

"Yeah. Sure. Good idea," the others agreed hurriedly.

"So which tunnel do we take?" asked Petra.

The kids had hollered Shawn's name into both openings but received no answer in return. Neither opening was appealing. Both were small, inky-black holes. The tunnel Craig had found, near the roof, was a cramped, shoulder-width hole, less than three feet high. Petra had stuck her arm in as far as she could and found that the passage followed a tight curve into the black unknown.

Colin's tunnel was worse.

"It doesn't even qualify as a tunnel!" Tony protested. He was right. It was more of a crack than a hole—a narrow gap between the floor of the cave and a huge slab of rock that had shifted when the earth was shrugging off the last of the ice-age glaciers thousands of years ago.

"At least we know where the water is going," Craig commented, pointing to the shallow, icy stream that bisected the cave floor. It vanished into the crack beneath the wall, disappearing into the subterranean darkness. Taking the low hole would mean a tight, freezing-wet belly crawl, sandwiched between a thousand-ton slab of rock and the glacial stream.

"Um, I vote for high and dry," said Tony. "Anyway, the higher tunnel is closer to the cave mouth. Maybe the rush of water and debris knocked Shawn in there when he jumped."

"It's possible, I guess," said Petra. She didn't like the look of the low, wet hole any better than Tony. "We'll take the higher tunnel," she decided. "If we hit a dead end, *then* we'll come back and try the lower tunnel."

—m—

Alone in the smothering darkness, Shawn blinked frantically, willing himself to see something, anything. He strained his eyes, trying to penetrate the solid, black shroud that had dropped over him.

But there was nothing.

The darkness pressed down on him like a weight, leaving him breathless. Panic swarmed and swirled inside his skull. Shawn took three deep breaths, forcing himself to breathe slowly.

It's like being lost in space, Shawn thought. Immediately, he was grateful for the sensation of the hard, wet boulder digging uncomfortably into his body. He pressed his hands against the rock's rough surface. It was proof that *something* existed in this cold, black vacuum—something solid, something real. Shawn was gripped by the sudden, irrational fear that if he let go of the rock, he might get sucked into the blackness and go orbiting away like an insignificant satellite.

Breathe, Shawn told himself. *Just breathe. You have four other senses—use them!*

Sliding forward on his boulder, Shawn felt for, and found, the edge of the rock. He lowered his feet cautiously and landed in a shallow puddle on a wet slab of rock. Holding his hands out in front of him, Shawn took a step forward. Then another. But on the third step, his foot found only emptiness. He flung his arms out but there was no wall to catch him and he pitched forward into space.

Shawn landed in water.

It closed briefly over his head before he came up again, spluttering and choking. He thrashed wildly, his heart constricted in terror. He'd had enough of water. More than enough. Then he touched bottom and realized he could stand. Shawn staggered to his feet and stood, shaking and gasping in ice-cold water that wasn't quite waist deep.

His fall, and his brief but panicked struggle with

the water, had disoriented him. He was no longer sure which way he was facing. Where had he been standing when he fell? Where was the edge of this underground pool? How big was it? Shawn stretched out his arms as far as they would reach. His exploring fingers touched only water.

Figures, he thought. He rotated his body a few degrees and reached out his hands once again. More water. Where was the bank of this underground lake? He turned slowly in a full circle, his palms skimming the surface of the strange, black pool. His fingers met nothing but water.

He squinted again, straining to pierce the darkness, but that was hopeless. The blackness was impenetrable. He shuffled forward a step, feeling the water sloshing around his thighs. He walked farther. And stopped, uncertain. Surely he hadn't fallen *that* far from the bank. And was it just his imagination, or was the water getting deeper? He took another step.

It was definitely getting deeper.

He must be heading towards the middle of the lake. Shawn stopped and began wading in a new direction. He kept his hands stretched out in front of him, expecting to touch a stone wall that would signal the end of the water. But his fingers found nothing. This must be a bigger cavern than he had realized.

Shawn stopped again. For all he knew, he could be walking parallel to the water's edge, just out of reach of the bank. He hesitated, then turned, angling in yet another direction. No, that wasn't right—the water was getting deeper again.

And it was paralyzingly cold.

He began to shiver.

"Petra!" he called. "Craig!" But the water and the surrounding stone swallowed the sound, smothering the words as soon as they left his mouth.

If only I could see! Shawn thought, and he slapped the water in frustration. The splash echoed in the darkness. And suddenly Shawn knew what to do.

Ducking under the water, Shawn ran his hands along the bottom, searching with his fingers. His hands closed on what he was looking for—a fist-sized rock. He stood back up, gasping with the cold. He tossed the rock out in front of him, a gentle, underhand throw. There was a gulping *plop* as the rock hit water.

"Okay, no dry land that way," muttered Shawn. He bobbed back down under the water and grabbed another rock. He shifted direction and again tossed a stone out into the darkness.

Splash!

He snatched up two more rocks. He let one fly.

Ker-splash!

Shawn rotated his body again. Holding his breath, he threw the last rock.

Thunk!

He had hit land! Shawn lunged towards the sound, splashing wildly through the water. He charged forward until he cracked his shin hard against a rocky ledge—and then he was hauling himself out of the water, shuddering with cold and relief.

Shawn crawled slowly across the shelf of rough, wet rock, feeling his way in the utter darkness. Water dripped from an unseen ceiling. Behind him the invisible lake gurgled sullenly against its stony banks. His exploring fingers met a wall. Running his hands along it, Shawn found an opening…the same tight tunnel in which he had almost drowned. It was emptied of water now…except for a glacial stream only a couple of inches deep. Probably the same spring we drank from outside, Shawn thought, in sudden surprise. Already the heat and light of the stone valley seemed a distant memory here in the damp, cold darkness. Shawn knelt, shivering and trembling at the tunnel's mouth. Running his fingers around the edge of the opening, he assessed its size. To fit inside, he would have to lie down on his belly in the stream and crawl forward on his elbows, sandwiched once again between water and stone. Claustrophobia closed around his heart like a vice. *I can't do it*, he thought.

—⚒—

"You know what's weird?" said Tony.

"What?" sighed Petra.

"For a White Cave, this place is pretty black."

"Can't argue with that," Colin admitted.

"It *would* look white if there was a bit more light

down here to reflect off the rock," Petra said. "This whole place is made out of gypsum."

Craig climbed the sloping cave wall and peered again into the small opening he had found near the ceiling.

"We're going to need a light if we want to go this way," he said, leaning into the hole. He slid back down the rocky incline to where the others were waiting. "It's pitch black in there. We're not going to be able to see a thing."

Petra turned and scrambled towards the cave mouth. "Come on, Tony," she ordered. "It's time to make a torch."

The Bat Cave

Scraping away dirt and rock with their fingernails, Tony and Petra finally managed to pull a thick branch loose from the debris plugging the cave mouth. Dragging it back to the others, Petra quickly stripped it of leaves and twigs.

"I need some cloth," she said.

With a sharp yank, Colin pulled off one of the sleeves from his plaid shirt and handed it to Petra.

"It's a bit damp," he said, "but not too bad."

Petra nodded and began winding the fabric around the top of the branch. Pulling her long ponytail loose, she used the hair elastic to secure the cloth in place. She looked at Colin expectantly.

"Matches?" she asked, holding out her hand.

Wordlessly, Colin dug into his front shirt pocket and pulled out a book of matches.

"How did you know he'd have matches?" demanded Tony.

"Nobody carries a pack of cigarettes without carrying something to light them with," said Petra shortly. "And Colin had cigarettes at the quarry."

"They're not mine. I don't smoke. I swiped them

from my stepdad," Colin muttered. "The guys told me to make sure to bring them some smokes."

"And look how well *that* turned out," said Tony darkly.

Petra sighed. "Well, we have matches and a torch, but we still need fuel. Otherwise the cloth will just burn right up and go out."

"You mean like kerosene or barbecue starter?" Craig asked. Petra nodded.

"We used gasoline last time," said Tony, remembering their dark and uncomfortable voyage on the Chocolate River. "Hey! The gas in Colin's ATV! We could use that!"

"You mean the ATV that's out in the middle of the forest and probably burned to a crisp by now?" asked Colin.

"Oh. Right."

Petra was digging through her pockets. She pulled out her tube of lip balm and looked at it, thoughtful.

"You look fine," Tony told her. "Is this really the time to worry about makeup?"

"It's not makeup," Petra huffed. "It's *moisturizer*. But I think it might also be the fuel we're looking for."

"Huh?" said the boys.

"Listen to these ingredients." Petra read aloud from the side of the tube: "Wax, cetyl alcohol, paraffin, mineral oil, camphor, petroleum."

"Ew—you put that stuff on your *lips*?" Craig

whistled and shook his head. "I will never understand girls."

"This stuff's for boys, too, you know," Petra told him.

"Not *this* boy!"

Petra pulled the cap off the tube and began smearing the lip balm over the cloth at the end of the torch.

"That's it," she said when the entire tube was empty. "Light it up."

Colin struck a match and held it to the wax-coated cloth. It hissed, spluttered, then flared with a *whoosh!* Petra held the torch aloft. It lit the cavern with a weird, flickering glow.

"Let's get moving," said Colin, starting toward the tunnel.

"Wait!" cried Craig suddenly. The others stopped and looked at him. "What if Shawn's not down this tunnel?" he said. "What if he comes looking for us and we're already gone?"

Petra stooped, and with her free hand, picked up a chunk of gypsum. Using the gypsum, she drew a large, white arrow on a slab of grey shale. Under the arrow, she wrote their initials: P, T, C & C.

"There," she said. "If Shawn comes this way, he'll know where we've gone."

Climbing up to the tunnel, she wormed her way carefully inside. The others followed.

The tunnel was tight. They wriggled forward on their hands and knees. The rocky walls of the narrow passage rubbed against their sides, scraping knees and elbows. More than once they bumped their heads on the low, uneven ceiling. The torch flickered dimly, casting crazy, leering shadows. In its light, white gypsum gleamed through the walls like bones in an ancient crypt. As they wormed their way around a tight corner, the tunnel suddenly widened.

"Hang on," said Petra. A jumble of boulders was lying across their path. At the top of the heap, two huge slabs of stone had toppled inwards, and stood leaning against each other.

Petra climbed up the rock pile. She ducked through the triangular opening beneath the two leaning rocks and vanished from sight. The others waited in the dark. The only sound was their breathing, echoing off the cold, damp walls. After a long moment, Petra's head reappeared again above the rock pile. "We can get through this way," she called. "Just watch your step once you come through—there's a bit of a drop."

The boys scrambled through the boulders and joined Petra on the other side.

"It seems like the tunnel gets wider here," she said, poking the torch into the shadowy gloom ahead.

"Our voices sound different, too," observed Craig. "More echoey or something."

"Hello hello!" Tony called into the looming darkness.

"*Helloooo—helloooo—helloooooooo…*" the echoes moaned back in ghostly voices.

"Tony! Cut that out!" hissed Petra.

"Why?" giggled Tony. "Who's gonna hear?"

"We don't want to disturb anything," said Petra, edging forward into the deeper dark.

"Disturb what? The rocks?" scoffed Tony. "Hey, rocks! Am I disturbing ya?" he called.

"*Ya-ya-ya...*" taunted the darkness.

"Knock it off, Tony," whispered Craig, nervously. "What if you wake something up?"

"Wake up what?" Tony demanded. "These caves are empty." He looked at Petra. "Right?"

Petra didn't say anything. She was peering ahead into the darkness.

"*Right*?" Tony persisted.

"Sure, Tony," said Petra, sarcastically. "I come down here every day just to make sure these caves are kept clean and critter-free, just for you. Now be quiet!" She moved carefully forward.

"Critters?" gulped Tony. "Nobody said anything about critters."

Petra shrugged. "Lots of animals take shelter in caves, Tony."

"Oh, man." Tony scuttled closer to her, looking nervously over his shoulder.

Petra edged her way around a rock column, slid down a tilted slab of rock, held up her torch and...

"*Whoa!*" breathed all four kids.

The flame's spluttering light illuminated the high, uneven walls of a huge cavern.

But the homemade torch wasn't nearly bright enough to dispel all the shadows. Darkness pooled in the corners and hung like a curtain from the ceiling. The floor was a giant jigsaw puzzle of stone slabs, and it sloped sharply upward towards the earthy roof at the far end of the cavern.

Petra moved towards the centre of the cavern, stepping over a crack in the floor.

"Shawn?" she called tentatively, holding out the torch.

No answer.

Craig's shoulders sagged. "He's not here." His voice ached with disappointment. Standing there in that cold and cavernous space, Craig suddenly looked very young.

Petra moved swiftly over to him and laid an arm across his shoulders. "Don't worry, Craig. I'm sure Shawn's fine. He's probably just looking for us, too." She tried to smile, but her own dismay welled up suddenly in her throat.

"I think I know where we are," said Colin, coming up behind them. "I've heard people talk about this place. We're in the Bat Cave."

"I don't see any Batmobile," said Tony, picking his way carefully across the uneven floor.

Colin shook his head. "Does this feel like a comic book to you, kid? I'm talking about *real* bats. Hundreds of 'em. They hibernate in here during the winter."

Petra glanced up at the shadows lurking near the roof. "Are they here now?" she whispered.

"I doubt it. They would have moved off into the forest for the summer."

There was a brief silence as they remembered what state the forest was in.

"Hey, I found something." Tony had been running his hands along one side of the cave. A crack opened up into a small niche off the main cavern. "There's something in here," said Tony, feeling around. He pulled out a handful of small, hard, round objects. "Hey! Look! Nuts!" He held them out to show the others. "Squirrels must have stashed them in here. There's tons of them! At least we won't starve." He opened his mouth.

"Tony, wait!" said Petra. She picked up one of the small objects and looked at it closely in the light of the torch. "Uh, I don't think you want to eat that."

"Huh? Why not?" asked Tony. "I like nuts."

"This isn't a nut."

"Sure it is," argued Tony. "It's round. It's hard. What else would it be?"

"Porcupine scat," said Petra, tossing the pellet back into the niche. She sniffed at the opening and wrinkled her nose. "I think you just found their indoor toilet."

"*Gah*!" Tony dropped his handful of pellets like a hot potato. "You mean I was about to eat *porcupine poo*?"

"I guess bats aren't the only critters who like to hang out in here," Craig commented as Tony went hopping away across the cavern, wiping his hands frantically on his shirt.

"Ew! Blah! Porcupine germs! I'm covered with porcupine germs!"

"Relax, Tony. I think you'll live," giggled Petra.

"Oh, man," moaned Tony. "This has been SUCH an uncool day."

Colin, meanwhile, was examining the far section of the cave, where floor and ceiling came together. Petra made her way up the sloping floor to where Colin was prying among the rocks under the roof of the cave. Tony followed, still muttering under his breath about the hygiene habits of porcupines. Petra knelt beside Colin, holding up the torch to chase away some of the shadows.

"Any sign of a way out?" Petra asked. But Colin shook his head.

"It seems pretty solid, except—"

Just then Craig pushed past Tony and tugged at Petra's sleeve.

"Hey," he whispered in an anxious voice. "I heard something moving behind those rocks over there." He pointed back down the cavern towards a shadowy corner not far from where they had entered the Bat Cave. They all turned toward the inky darkness at the bottom of the cave.

"You probably just *thought* you heard something,"

said Tony. But Craig shook his head vigorously.

"You're sure you heard something?" Petra asked in a low voice. Craig nodded.

Petra raised the torch and moved slowly down the tilted stone floor. The boys followed, cautious. When she was halfway across the cavern, she stopped and held out the torch. Its feeble light didn't penetrate the black shadows lurking behind the rubble of rocks and boulders at the bottom of the cave.

There was a rattle of small stones.

"Shawn? Is that you?" Petra called out in a small voice. She took a step closer.

There was another rattle of rocks, followed by a short, choking cough.

"Sh-Shawn?" Petra stabbed the torch in the direction of the darkest shadow. Something *was* moving down there. There was a rustling…the sound of something shifting, turning, and then:

Two red eyes flashed open, glowing with demonic brightness in the torchlight.

What's Big and Black and Shaggy All Over?

"Hobart!" exclaimed Tony, catching sight of a shiny, wet nose and a black, furry muzzle beneath the glowing eyes. "It's Hobie! He found us!"

He ducked past Petra and scooted down the slanting floor towards the den of tumbled boulders against the back wall. There was a scrabbling of claws on rock and the eyes and nose vanished behind the rock pile.

"Hobart! Here, boy! Are you hurt?" Tony called. He whistled encouragingly.

"Tony—" said Petra.

"C'mere, boy!" coaxed Tony, picking his way awkwardly over the rocks. "Don't be scared—it's just us."

There was a chuffing cough from the darkness behind the boulders.

"Sounds like Hobart's suffering from smoke inhalation," said Tony, worriedly. "We should get him checked out by the vet when we get out of here."

"Tony—" said Colin. But Tony was already stretching his hand into the dark space behind the rocks.

"Hobie? Where are you, boy? It's okay…you're safe now. Come on out." Tony craned his head awkwardly around the rock pile. "Ah, there you are. Wow, what big paws you have. And claws. Geez, Petra, don't you ever trim Hobie's nails?" Tony coughed. "Phew! And he needs a bath, too!" He backed out of the dark space and looked up at the others. "What are you guys still doing up there? Don't you want to come down here and see Hobie?"

"Tony," Craig whispered hoarsely, "I don't think that's Hobart!"

"What are you talking about?" scoffed Tony, turning to look up at his friends. "Of course it's Hobart. Who else do we know that's big and black and shaggy?"

As Tony spoke, a big, black, and shaggy shape slowly emerged from the shadows behind him.

"T-T-T-T-Tony…" stammered Craig.

Petra was opening and closing her mouth, but no sound was coming out. Colin raised his hand and pointed, staring past Tony with horror-filled eyes.

"What the heck is the matter with you guys?" asked Tony, looking up at them. "I never saw anybody act so weird over a dog!"

"N-n-not a d-dog, Tony," gasped Petra. "B-b-b-b…"

Tony wrinkled his brow in confusion. "Huh?"

"B-b-b-b-*behind you*!"

Tony blinked at Petra. Slowly, he turned—and

looked up, up, up at the big and black and shaggy shape towering over him.

"BEAR!!!!" howled Tony.

The bear opened its jaws, revealing a huge mouthful of gleaming teeth.

RRRRRRROARRRRRRRR!!!!

"AAAAAAAHHHHHHHHH!!!!"

The bear swung a sledgehammer paw at Tony, but Tony was already gone. Quick as a cricket, he went leaping across the cave and ducked behind Petra.

"B-b-b-b…" he quaked. "Not a d-d-d-…"

"We know, Tony," breathed Petra.

Below them, the bear dropped down on all four paws. It swung its head back and forth, rocking its heavy body from side to side. Clinging together, the four young people backed slowly away until they were wedged against the low roof of the cave at the far end of the cavern. Below them, the bear huffed and snorted. A patch of raw and blistered skin cut a painful-looking stripe across the animal's flank—a souvenir from a burning branch and evidence of the bear's narrow escape from the fire.

"What do we do?" croaked Craig, his eyes fixed on the agitated animal.

"Black bears aren't usually aggressive towards people," Colin whispered, "unless they're wounded or cornered."

"You mean like that one down there?" hissed Petra.

Colin nodded, staring wide-eyed as the bear

suddenly lashed out furiously at a pile of rubble, sending a bowling ball–sized rock smashing against the cave wall. The bear lifted his head and roared.

"We're invading his space," whispered Colin. "He doesn't like that."

"I don't like it either!" Craig whispered back.

"Hey, man, he can *have* his space," chattered Tony. "I don't want anything to do with his space!"

"He's blocking the only exit," whispered Petra, nodding to the shadowy tunnel behind the bear. "We need another way out of here."

Colin nodded. "I thought I felt something in the corner up here…" Cautiously, he edged towards the right. Keeping an eye on the swaying, pacing bear below him, Colin stretched out his hand to reach behind a jagged piece of gypsum jutting out from the wall.

"There's an alcove back here," he whispered to Petra. He grunted as he stretched his arm farther into the cramped space. "There's a little ledge behind this rock…and there's some space above it. Can't see how high it goes. I—I can feel some tree roots hanging down."

"How big is the space?" Petra whispered back. "Can we all fit in?"

Colin shook his head.

"No. There's maybe room enough for one person. One *small* person," he added, nodding significantly towards Craig.

"Oh. Right." Petra leaned over to Craig.

"Craig," she said quietly, "I want you to move over by Colin. Do it slowly and quietly. There's a little space behind the rock that you can climb into. The bear won't be able to reach you there." *I hope*, she thought.

"What about you guys?" Craig whispered back.

"Don't worry about us. We'll find a way to distract the bear. Then we'll all leave together."

Craig's mouth set in a stubborn line. "No way," he hissed. "I'm not going to hide while you guys take on a bear!"

"Craig!" Petra pleaded. "Please. Get in there! It's the safest place!"

"*No!*" Craig hissed back.

"Petra," interrupted Colin. "Let me see the torch for a minute. I want to check something."

Petra passed him the spluttering, fading torch. Colin took it and held it inside the little alcove. "I still think I can feel something…" He lifted the torch higher into the dark space behind the rock.

A breath of air—a stray breeze—came sighing out of the darkness of the alcove. It curled playfully around the last feeble flames on the torch…and snuffed them out.

"Well, *this* isn't good," said Tony.

Battle in the White Caves

"*What did you do*?!" exclaimed Petra in a strangled whisper.

"Nothing!" Colin's voice came back out of the darkness. "There was a breeze!"

The darkness was as thick as tar.

"This is bad," moaned Tony. "Bad, bad, bad…"

"Be quiet," hissed Craig's voice. "We need to *listen*."

For a few seconds, they could hear only their rapid breathing and their own hearts pounding in their ears. Petra held her breath, listening.

Even her *skin* seemed to be listening. She could feel the hair on her arms and on the back of her neck rising like tiny radio antennas.

Somewhere in front of them, a pebble rolled and knocked against another pebble. A tiny sound, it was magnified a hundred times by their fear. Was it the bear? Was it coming towards them? There was a low, chuffing cough in the blackness, and then the sound of heavy claws clicking against stone.

"Oh, man. We're playing Blind Man's Bluff with a bear," Tony moaned quietly. "Except that *everybody's* blind!"

"Not the bear," Craig whispered. "He has his sense of smell. And he's used to moving around in dark caves."

"Are you trying to make me feel better?" whispered Tony. "Because it's not working."

"Colin," breathed Petra, "can you light the torch again?"

She heard a faint rustling from her right. There was a brief scuffling sound and then something slapped lightly against the rock floor.

"Shoot," whispered Colin. "I dropped the matches."

An irritable coughing grunt sounded from the darkness below.

"Shhhh," said Petra. "Try again."

There was more rustling, then—

"Found them!" whispered Colin.

Petra heard the sound of the matchbook being folded back. Then a match snapped and flared, sizzling loudly in the thick, black quiet of the cavern. At once, the bear bellowed angrily. In the flickering light, they saw it rear up on its hind legs, pawing viciously at the air.

"I don't think it likes fire!" squeaked Craig.

"Light the torch! Light the torch!" urged Petra.

With a shaking hand, Colin held the match to the small scrap of singed cloth still clinging to the stick.

It went out.

A series of low, angry grunts were now coming from the bear's direction. There was a clatter of stones.

"He's coming this way!" gasped Petra. "Hurry, light the torch!"

"No—you'll only make him angry!" said Craig.

"We have to know where he is," protested Petra.

"I don't *want* to know where he is!" moaned Tony.

There was another loud snap and a brief flare as Colin struck a second match. The flame flickered and gained strength. In its light, the bear's eyes shone with a ghostly gleam. The animal was now halfway up the sloping floor and coming straight towards them.

Colin held the match to the homemade torch. "Please catch," he breathed. "Please, please catch!"

A spark chewed reluctantly at the scrap of cloth with a sulky, sullen glow, but it refused to catch.

The match burned down to Colin's fingers. He dropped it. It sizzled against the stone floor and went out. Immediately, Colin struck another and held it again to the branch. This time, the flame licked at the stick aggressively—and caught! The flame bit into the wood, cloning itself into a flickering army of blue-centred soldiers that clawed and stabbed at the darkness.

Colin thrust the torch out in front of him like a sword. "YAH!" he hollered. "Get back!!"

The bear bellowed, tossing his head like an angry bull.

"Craig!" yelled Petra. "Get into the alcove. *Now.*"

"But—" started Craig.

The bear bellowed again and gave the stone floor a thunderous slap with a massive paw.

"Well okay, then," said Craig hastily. "Since you

insist!" He turned and scrambled behind the white boulder, disappearing into the alcove.

"This torch isn't going to last," gasped Colin. "There's barely any cloth left at the top—just the branch itself is burning. I'm going to have to drop it soon."

"Isn't there anything else we can light?" asked Petra, desperately scanning the ground around her feet. But there was only stone.

They had their backs pressed against the wall now.

In front of them, the bear swayed menacingly and took another step forward. It roared again.

"There has to be another way out of here!" said Tony.

Colin looked at him. A strange expression suddenly crossed his face. "Tony, you're a genius!"

"Huh?" Tony blinked at Colin. "Who? *Me*?"

"You're right—there *does* have to be another way out of here!" Colin said excitedly. "A breeze blew the torch out. A *breeze*! It had to come from somewhere. It had to come from *outside*!" He turned and leaned into the alcove. He called up into the darkness.

"Craig! Feel around with your hands. Is there a hole in the ceiling?"

There was a scuffling and a scrabbling in the shadows behind the stone.

"I don't know," came Craig's voice. "Hang on…"

"Hang on? *Hang on*? We don't have *time* to hang on!" squawked Tony.

The bear humped its massive body up the stone slab towards them. It stopped a few short metres away, snarling.

"Yes! Yes! There *is* a hole!" came Craig's excited voice. "I think we're under a tree. I can see some light…there's a small hole between the roots!"

"How small, Craig?"

"Pretty small—but I might be able to loosen the earth around it!"

"Then make like a beaver and get busy!" yelped Tony. "We're running out of time down here!"

From the alcove came the sound of scraping and digging. A shower of earth and gravel fell down from the behind the boulder.

"I'm almost through!" came Craig's muffled voice.

"Hurry! *Keep digging*!" urged Colin, waving the smouldering branch at the advancing bear. The bear flattened its ears furiously against its skull and swatted at the flaming branch. Colin skipped sideways, but the bear was faster. A swipe of its paw sent the boy sprawling across the rocky floor. The torch fell from Colin's limp hand and rolled down the sloped floor until it stopped against a rock at the bottom of the cave. Petra leaped towards Colin, but her movement caught the attention of the bear. The animal whirled towards her with a ferocious snarl.

"Get back, you overgrown rodent!" Tony yelled, bounding to Petra's side and holding up both his fists like a boxer. "Come on!" he cried, bouncing on the balls of his feet. "Give me your best shot!"

RRRRRRRROARRRRR!!

The bear's rancid breath ruffled Tony's brush cut.

"Okay, well, maybe not your *best* shot," gulped Tony.

At that moment a muffled yell came from the alcove.

"Craig?" cried Petra in alarm.

She started to move towards the alcove, but a paw, spiked with lethal-looking claws, slammed into the cave wall beside her, pulling down a mini-landslide of rock and soil. The paw rose again.

Petra shrieked in terror.

"Get back!" Tony yelled. Bouncing forward, he punched the bear squarely in the nose. With a roar of rage, the bear swatted Tony as if he were an annoying insect, knocking him into the shadows.

The bear swivelled back to Petra. Eyes locked on the bear, Petra reached down, fumbling frantically around the floor. Her fingers closed around a small rock. She threw it at the bear. The little stone bounced harmlessly off its thick, black hide. Petra bent to pick up another rock. The bear reared above her. Petra pressed her back against the wall of the cave and shut her eyes.

At that instant, a sound came from the darkness down below. It started as a low, ghostly moan and swelled into a buzzing wail that grew and grew until the entire cave seemed to vibrate with the noise.

The bear whirled to face this new, unknown foe.

In the dying glow of the torch, the silhouette of a boy could be just seen, standing at the tunnel's mouth at the bottom of the cave. He was swinging something around and around his head.

WHIRRRRR-WHIRRRRR-WHIRRRRRR-WHIRRRRRR!

The noise buzzed like a swarm of mutant mosquitoes. The bear bawled in fury.

"Shawn!" screamed Petra. "Look out!"

With a roar, the bear charged.

Shawn waited until the bear had almost reached him...then he let the bullroarer go. It sliced through the air, catching the bear hard just below the ear. The bear bawled in surprise and jerked backwards, sitting down hard on its haunches. Shawn scrambled sideways, snatching up the still-smouldering torch. The bear huffed menacingly towards him, shaking its head in irritation.

"Shawn! Get up here!" cried Petra.

Shawn ducked a swinging paw and stabbed at the bear's gaping mouth with the burning branch. The bear bawled again and leaped backwards, snarling and clacking its teeth. Dodging past the distracted animal, Shawn sprinted up the slope towards Petra.

"Are you okay? Where's Craig?" he demanded breathlessly, grabbing her by the shoulders.

"Craig went up there, but I don't know what happened to him!" gasped Petra, pointing to the dark space behind the gypsum boulder. Shawn lunged towards the hidden alcove.

Below them, the bear gave a throaty growl and began to stalk towards them.

"Craig!" Shawn was hollering frantically into the dark space behind the rock.

No answer.

"Shawn, the bear's coming!" cried Petra.

Shawn pulled his head out of the alcove. He turned towards the shuffling, snarling animal and brandished what was left of the torch. Still the bear advanced. Raising his arms high, Shawn threw back his head and yelled.

"*WAAHHHHHHHH*!!!"

The bear hesitated. It rocked back a step, curling its lips over a set of dangerous-looking teeth.

"*WAAAAAAHHHHHHH*!" Shawn yelled again, taking a step forward.

Another roar thundered out of the shadows—but it didn't come from the bear.

It didn't come from Shawn, either.

It came from the black space above the alcove.

There was a frantic scrabbling, and then a shower of earth and gravel suddenly cascaded down from above. A second later, a big, black, shaggy body exploded out of the alcove. It charged past Shawn, knocking him sideways against Petra, and raced down the cavern floor towards the startled bear.

"HOBART!" yelled Petra and Shawn together.

The Newfoundland didn't even break stride. He flew at the bear, his thunderous, bass battle cry rippling from his throat.

This proved to be too much for the bear. With a frightened bawl, it whirled and bolted down the tunnel, with the enraged dog snarling and snapping at its heels.

Petra and Shawn were left gaping in shock at the place where the animals had vanished.

Before they could say anything, a brilliant white light punched a hole in the darkness above the alcove, and voices were calling their names.

Hellos and Goodbyes

The flashing lights of the emergency vehicles reflected off the low, smoky clouds, lending a disco-ball dazzle to the eerie glow of the twilight sky. Petra sat on the bumper of an ambulance, trying to convince her Uncle Daryl that she was okay.

"Really, I'm *fine*," she told him for the seventeenth time. "Just some scrapes and bruises."

But Daryl insisted she wear the oxygen mask for a while longer, anyway—just to clean the smoke out of her lungs, he said.

Petra tried to breathe slowly and deeply as she sifted through the chaotic memories from the past hour. It was a bit of a blur. The images were jumbled and, she suspected, not entirely in order. She remembered Hobart bursting out of the alcove and chasing the bear. She remembered seeing Tony knocked aside like a rag doll. And Colin. What had happened to them? Craig had vanished up the hole like Alice in Wonderland. And then Shawn, appearing out of nowhere. Standing up to the bear, yelling like a demented warrior. Shawn, swinging the bullroarer in the glow of the torch. And a light shining down through the dark. Shouts. Hands reaching down through a hole above the alcove, pulling her and Shawn back up into the light.

Back into the world.

And then strong arms carrying them through a skeleton-forest of charred and smoking trees…

Fire trucks, police cars, and ambulances lined the country road. Petra watched in the twilight as firefighters moved methodically through the burnt-over woods, hosing down still-smouldering brush and checking for hot spots. EMS personnel spoke into radios and walkie-talkies, communicating with emergency workers and volunteers in other areas of the burn site.

Two paramedics walked briskly towards another ambulance, pushing a gurney. The outline of a body lay motionless beneath the blanket. Petra caught a glimpse of bristly brown hair poking out from the edge of the sheet. Tearing off her oxygen mask, she raced over to the stretcher.

"Tony!" She grabbed the side of the gurney and yanked back the sheet. Tony's white face stared up at her. "Hey, watch it!" he complained. "Injured dude coming through here!"

"Tony!" cried Petra. "Are you okay?"

Tony moaned dramatically and rolled his eyes back in his head. "I think this is the end. Everything's… going…dark. Petra!" Tony's eyes suddenly focused and he snatched at Petra's sleeve.

"What is it?" Petra asked, startled.

"I just want you to know, I'm leaving my iPod to you," Tony told her in a sorrowful voice. "Shawn gets my game system. Craig can have my trading card collection. Think of me when you use them."

"Tony," Petra began, a smile playing on her lips. "I don't think—"

"No, no," said Tony, waving his hand, feebly. "Don't argue. My most valuable possessions should go to my best friends."

"But Tony," said Petra. "I really think you're going to be—"

Tony flopped back on the pillow. "I see a light," he whispered, putting his hand to his forehead. "Does anyone else see the pretty light? Must…go… to the light. I hear music…and someone calling my name…"

"Uh, Tony? The pretty light is coming from the fire trucks," Petra told him matter-of-factly. "The music is from Daryl's truck radio and I do believe that's Craig calling your name."

"Tony!" gasped Craig, rushing up. "What's wrong with him?" he asked, turning to the paramedics. "Is he dying?"

"Just a broken collarbone. He'll be fine in a week or two," a paramedic said kindly. She smiled and patted Tony's fuzzy head.

"Hey—watch the hair!" protested Tony. "Show a little respect for the Boy Who Boxed a Bear and

Lived!" Tony glanced sideways at Petra. "Do you think they'll make a movie about me?" he asked.

"Sure," giggled Petra. "And Oprah will probably want to interview you, too."

"Oh *yeah*," said Tony, nodding seriously. "You're probably right!"

Petra turned and almost bumped into Shawn, who had come up behind her and was standing there quietly. He had a blanket draped around his shoulders. His right hand was bandaged and resting in a sling. There was a nasty scrape on his cheekbone, and the gash over his eye was bleeding.

"Hey," he said.

"Shawn!" said Petra, throwing her arms around him. She took a step back and looked at him critically. "You look awful."

Shawn gave her a lopsided smile. "I'm okay. Are *you* all right?"

"Sure," she said.

"I got your message," Shawn said. "Back there in the cave. That was good thinking."

"I don't know about that," said Petra, shaking her head ruefully. "When I drew that arrow, I didn't think I'd be leading you straight to an angry bear. I just wanted you to be able to find us."

"It worked," said Shawn.

"You found us just in time," said Petra with a shiver.

"But how did you make that crawl in the total dark?" Craig wanted to know.

"Very carefully," said Shawn. "I remembered that we have more senses than just sight, so I followed the sound of your voices. And I held a stick out in front of me to help me feel where the tunnel was going. Still managed to bump my head on the ceiling, though." He touched his bloody forehead and winced.

The blanket had slipped from one of Shawn's shoulders. Petra reached up and gently tugged the blanket back up around his neck. "You're soaked!" she exclaimed as her hand touched his wet collar.

"Uh, yeah," said Shawn, sheepishly. "I sort of fell in an underground lake."

He was shivering, Petra realized. Shawn started to say something else, but suddenly he swayed on his feet.

"Whoa, there!" said Craig, grabbing his brother's elbow.

"Easy!" said Petra, slipping her arm around Shawn's waist as he sagged between them. They eased him into a sitting position on the edge of Tony's gurney just as an annoyed-looking paramedic came jogging over to them.

"*There* you are!" the paramedic exclaimed crossly, wagging a stern finger at Shawn. "You're supposed to be lying down in that ambulance over there being treated for shock and exposure!"

"I had to check on my friends," protested Shawn through chattering teeth, but he allowed himself to be led back over to the waiting ambulance.

Craig shook his head in mock exasperation. "Leave it to my big brother to come out of a forest fire with hypothermia," he said with a snort. "Yeesh!"

"Shawn's one of a kind," said Petra quietly.

Craig nudged Petra's arm. "Hey, check it out. Looks like the police finally caught up with those goons from the quarry." Craig pointed.

A short distance away, a police cruiser was parked alongside a couple of mud-spattered ATVs. Two officers stood talking to the teenaged drivers. One of the teens looked scared. The other looked angry. As the police officers ushered the boys into the back seat of the cruiser, the angry teen protested loudly, pointing repeatedly at an ambulance parked across the road.

On a gurney next to the ambulance lay a boy.

"Colin!" gasped Petra.

The two large RCMP officers strode over to Colin's stretcher. They spoke to him in serious voices while Colin looked up at them with large, frightened eyes. Then one of the officers bent over Colin and snapped something on his wrist.

Petra gasped in disbelief. "They just handcuffed him to the stretcher!" Leaving Craig, Petra hurried towards the ambulance.

The officer signalled the paramedics, who began lifting the stretcher into the ambulance. Petra rushed over and grabbed the policeman's arm.

"What are you doing?" she demanded. "Colin's not

a criminal. He *helped* us! He saved our lives!"

The officer looked down at her sternly. "Starting
a fire is a very serious offense, young lady. A forest
was destroyed. Firefighters risked their lives today…"
The policeman shook his head. "We have received
information that this boy was involved in starting the
fire. If that's true, he must face the consequences of
the law."

The officer turned and climbed into the ambulance
next to Colin. Petra tugged at the paramedic's sleeve.

"Is he going to be okay?" she asked. "The boy, I
mean—Colin? Is he badly hurt?"

"He's got some cuts and bruises and a few cracked
ribs, but he'll be all right." The paramedic shut the
ambulance doors. The sirens wailed mournfully as
the vehicle pulled away. Through its bright back
window, Petra could see the big policeman sitting
sternly and silently beside Colin's slight and lonely
form.

"Petra!"

Her Uncle Daryl was calling her, waving her back
over to the ambulance. Petra walked slowly over to
him. Suddenly she felt exhausted. Every bone in her
body ached.

"I think you better sit down," Uncle Daryl said,
eyeing her critically. "You look just about done in."
He opened the back door of the ambulance and held
out his hand to help her inside. Petra sighed. She was
too tired to protest. She climbed into the ambulance

and was about to flop down on the stretcher when she noticed it was already occupied.

Hobart was stretched out on his back, with all four paws in the air. He wore an oxygen mask too, over his black snout, and looked rather embarrassed about the whole thing. He blinked sheepishly at Petra from behind the mask and thumped his tail apologetically.

"Hobart!" Petra cried, throwing her arms around him and burying her face in the shaggy neck. "My hero!"

The black tail drummed enthusiastically against the stretcher. Hobart rolled over and pushed his head under her chin, trying his best to lick her through the oxygen mask. Uncle Daryl chuckled and gently removed the mask. "I think you're going to be just fine, pal," he said, ruffling the big dog's floppy ears. Hobart burped affectionately and leaned against him, drooling contentedly down the front of Daryl's jacket.

"You should have seen him, Uncle Daryl," Petra said, looking at the big dog wonderingly. "It was like a werewolf exploded out of the dark down there. He went after that bear like it was just some overgrown cat!"

Daryl shook his head with an amused smile. "I guess we can add 'bears' to the list of things Hobie doesn't like," he said.

"Yeah! No kidding," said Petra. She paused. "Um… what *else* doesn't Hobart like? If he's going to morph into the Incredible Hobie, again, I want to be prepared."

Daryl scratched his head. "Well, now that you mention it, I can't think of anything else Hobie doesn't like. Except maybe broccoli."

"Bears and broccoli," said Petra, nodding seriously. "Got it." She thumped Hobart on the back. "You are some bodyguard," she told him.

"How did he find us?" Petra asked her uncle.

Daryl chuckled, wonderingly. "He just came tearing out of the woods and ran over to the fire trucks, barking like a maniac. Then he turned around and bolted straight back into the forest. It was the craziest thing. We went after him, but he wouldn't let us catch him… kept just ahead of us, barking like a fool the whole time. Then he ran over to this one tree and started nosing around. That's when we saw a hand coming up right out of the ground. *That* gave us quite a start, I can tell you!"

"It was Craig!" exclaimed Petra, "digging his way up through the roof of the Bat Cave!"

Daryl nodded. "We hauled Craig out of there and it was a few minutes before anybody noticed that Hobart was digging his way down into the hole. We looked up just in time to see his tail disappear. And you know what happened after that."

Petra shivered. She remembered.

"What happened to the bear?" she asked.

"Hobart must have chased it deep into the caves. All I know is, he came back all tuckered out but very pleased with himself, just as we were carrying Tony and that other boy out of the cave."

"Colin," said Petra. "His name's Colin. Where's the bear now?"

"Probably still holed up down there. I hear the rangers are going to try and tranquilize it tomorrow. They'll check the animal for injuries, give it some antibiotics, and release it far away from the burn site."

"Good," said Petra. "He'll have a healthy forest to live in again. Poor bear—it's not *his* fault that he was so cranky. I'd feel the same way if somebody burned *my* house down!"

A paramedic poked his head inside the ambulance. "Daryl, the other ambulances are ready to roll, but the boys won't let them leave until they know if Petra is going to meet them at the hospital."

Petra grinned. "Of course I'll be there. They're my best friends. Besides, *somebody* has to keep an eye on them. Those guys could find trouble at a knitting convention for retired safety inspectors." She hopped down from the stretcher and headed for Uncle Daryl's truck.

"Let's go!" she called over her shoulder. "We'd better get to the hospital before Tony accidentally demolishes the ER!"

New Beginnings

"So, Uncle D, where are we going?" asked Tony, leaning over the seat of Uncle Daryl's pickup.

Five weeks had passed and the summer had ripened into long, languid days washed with brilliant blue skies. Breezes rich with the smell of purple clover and new-mown hay unfurled through the open window as the red and black Ford growled along the narrow country road. Daryl smiled into the rearview mirror at the three boys crammed into the back seat.

"It's a surprise," he said.

"Aw, come on…give us a hint!" wheedled Craig.

"We're going to see a friend."

"But we don't know anybody who lives way out here," protested Petra, gazing out the passenger window at the remote, rural landscape flashing by outside. She shifted her shoulder out from under Hobart's drooling jowls. The amiable Newfoundland sighed loudly and slumped forward to rest his chin on the dashboard instead.

"What's that place?" asked Shawn suddenly, pointing through the front windshield as the truck crested a hill. Below them, in the distance, a patchwork quilt of paddocks and pastures sprawled out from a loose collection of barns and buildings. As they approached, several pens and wire-mesh enclosures came into view. They seemed to house a bewildering assortment of animals.

"Is that some kind of zoo?" Petra wondered aloud.

"It's a bit out of the way for a tourist attraction," murmured Shawn as they drew closer.

The answer came when Daryl pulled through the front gate. A wooden sign hung from the chain-link fence. It read: Atlantic Wildlife Rescue and Rehabilitation Refuge.

"What does *that* mean?" asked Tony. Daryl didn't answer, but pulled up in front of the main building and shut off the engine. The kids tumbled out of the truck. Just as they did, a man in a ranger's uniform came out of one of the barns. Seeing them, he hurried over and shook Daryl's hand heartily.

"Daryl! Good to see you again!"

"You too, Paul," replied Daryl, returning the handshake with a warm grin.

"Have you brought me some volunteers?" the ranger asked, winking at the kids.

"I'm sure they'd be happy to lend a hand," said Daryl. "But we really came to see how your new recruit is working out."

"Ah, yes," said Paul, nodding. "The boy. You know, that kid has been putting in some real long hours around here. Far more than required, actually. He definitely has a way with the animals. He's in Barn Three if you'd like to say hi." Paul waved them in the general direction. "Now if you'll excuse me, I've got to run. There's a stray moose calf causing a bit of a ruckus over in Sackville." Paul hopped into a green truck. The truck was hooked up to a rather battered-looking livestock trailer. Truck and trailer rattled through the gate with a cheerful honk of the horn.

Petra turned to Uncle Daryl with her hands on her hips. "Okay. Explain," she ordered.

Uncle Daryl chuckled and began leading them along a well-worn path. "Paul runs this place. He and his volunteers rescue lost and injured animals and look after them until they can be returned to the wild." Uncle Daryl nodded towards a cage holding a raccoon with a bandaged paw. "Sometimes when we're fighting forest fires, we find animals that have been hurt or disoriented by the blaze. This is where we bring them."

Shawn paused briefly by a high, wire-mesh cage. A great horned owl sat perched on a stump. It swivelled its head around, fixing Shawn with a hypnotic, unblinking stare. Next door to the owl, two crows cawed accusingly at them as they passed. Across from the crows, a timid red fox peeked out at them from inside a hollow log.

"Here we are," said Daryl, pointing at a red barn with a white number three painted on the door. Petra looked at her uncle questioningly. "Well, go on in,"

urged Daryl. "I'll wait for you back at the truck."
With that, he turned on his heel and strode back down
the path.

"What's this about?" wondered Shawn.

Petra shrugged. "No idea."

"Come on," said Craig, pushing the door open.
"Let's check it out."

"Are we sure there are no bears in here?" asked
Tony.

After the bright sunshine, the barn seemed dim and
shadowy. They stood still for a moment, waiting for
their eyes to adjust. An earthy, musky smell filled the
air, mingled with the sweeter aroma of hay. There
was a rustling noise and a voice called, "Who's
there?"

Shawn moved towards an open stall door. He
peered inside. Sitting on a bale of straw was Colin. In
his arms was a fawn.

The others crowded into the stall behind Shawn.

"Colin!" Petra started to exclaim, but the older boy
put a finger to his lips. He nodded at the wide-eyed
wild baby on his lap.

"Oh—sorry!" whispered Petra. Quietly, Colin
reached down and picked up a bottle of milk. He
offered it to the fawn and the young deer sucked at it
enthusiastically.

"So…what are you doing here?" Colin asked, his
eyes wary.

"What are *you* doing here?" demanded Tony. Colin

looked down at the fawn. "Making things right," he said. "As much as I can, anyway."

"I thought they threw you in the slammer," said Tony, suspicious.

"*Tony!*" hissed Petra.

"*What?*" said Tony.

"It's okay," Colin said to Petra. "They didn't throw me in the slammer," he told Tony. "Although maybe they should have. The judge sent me to counselling instead…and then he sent me to work here."

"Wow," said Petra. She reached out and touched a finger to the velvety neck of the fawn. "Do you like it?"

A smile spread across Colin's face. "It's the best job in the world," he said simply. The fawn finished its bottle and began nuzzling hungrily in Colin's armpit for more. Chuckling, Colin set the little creature gently down on its spindly legs and got to his own feet. The fawn tottered off to another corner of the stall and nosed around busily in the straw. The young people watched it in silence for a minute. Colin said quietly, "I've decided to study wildlife biology in school. I want to be a ranger like Paul and work with wild animals that need help. I—I want to try and make things better than they are," he said, glancing at Petra. The fawn wobbled back over to Colin and butted up against his knees. Colin reached down and rubbed the baby's wide, fuzzy ears.

"Looks like you're making quite a difference already," Petra told him.

"So what happened to the other guys?" asked Craig. "The bozos with the ATVs?"

Colin's eyes crinkled with wry amusement. "The judge assigned them to a different work detail— they're replanting trees over the entire burn site. They should be finished in another year or so."

"*Sweet*," said Craig with a wicked grin. "I hope the mosquitoes and blackflies are out in full force."

"Count on it," said Colin with a knowing smile. "Those Hillsborough hills are famous for breeding the most bloodthirsty insects for miles around."

Shawn cleared his throat. "I, uh, didn't get a chance to thank you after the fire," he said awkwardly. "We probably wouldn't have gotten out of those woods without you."

But Colin waved this off. "Naw," he said, "if I hadn't shown you the White Caves, I get the feeling that you would have just done something else...like build a hang-glider out of bubblegum and shoelaces or something."

Petra's laughter pealed through the barn. "Yep, that would be Shawn, all right!"

Shawn felt himself blushing scarlet, but before he could say anything in his own defence, Petra had hooked her arm through his elbow and was towing him back out into the sunshine.

"Come on, Colin," she called over her shoulder. "Give us the grand tour...then tell us what we can do to help."

"Yeah, great idea!" exclaimed Craig. "I want a closer look at that owl—he's got claws like a velociraptor!" He hurried out after Petra and his brother.

"You…you guys want to *help* me?" asked Colin, looking at Tony uncertainly. "Really?"

"Sure," said Tony, clapping a surprised Colin on the back. "That's what real friends do, you know. Just one thing, though…"

"What's that?"

"Don't ask me to clean up any porcupine poo," said Tony, shuddering. "Blech!"

"Fair enough," laughed Colin. "I've got a better job for you, anyway," he added, looking at his watch.

"Really? What?" asked Tony.

"It's time to feed Big Bertha."

"Big Bertha?" gulped Tony.

"Bertha…our black bear," said Colin, with a wicked grin.

Tony went rigid. "B-b-b-b-b…?" he stammered.

"Buddy," said Colin, throwing a friendly arm around his shoulder, "after all we've been through, this will be a walk in the park. I promise."

And whistling happily, Colin picked up a bucket and strolled outside…where his friends were waiting for him.

The places in this book really do exist. As a child,
I spent much time exploring the beautiful woods
and trails of Hillsborough, New Brunswick. The old
gypsum quarries were an awesome (albeit dangerous)
playground. My friends and I played hide-and-seek
among the piles of white boulders, and rode our bikes
and ponies through the abandoned gravel pits. We
ranged along the rugged clifftops and slid down their
white, scree-covered slopes. Today, these hills and
quarries are known as the White Rock Recreation Area.

The White Caves were formed at the end of the
ice age when melting glaciers washed away large
deposits of gypsum. They are part of a delicate
ecosystem and should be treated with care and
respect. *Never* go into a cave without permission
and *always* seek the advice and guidance of a
knowledgeable caving expert. Professional guides
keep both visitors and the caves safe from harm.
NEVER, EVER draw or write on cave walls. This
is called graffiti, and it is a very damaging form of
vandalism. In this book, I also use some creative
licence when describing the interior layout and
features of the cave. The "White Cave" in this story
is really a composite of different caves found in the
Hillsborough and Albert County area.

Happy adventuring!

—*Jennifer McGrath Kent*

ACKNOWLEDGEMENTS

I am deeply indebted to the following people for their contributions to the creative processes that went into the writing of this book: Richard and Kathy Faulkner of Baymount Outdoor Adventures for guiding me so expertly through the White Caves and for being a wealth of information; Harold McQuade and Orienteering New Brunswick for providing me with detailed maps of the White Rock area of Hillsborough and for giving me the opportunity to become well and thoroughly lost in those same woods; Deborah Carr, who cheerfully volunteered to wander around with me in the Pits of Despair; Will Lawrence, friend, fellow X-Grad, and volunteer firefighter, for recounting his experiences of forest fires with the Maitland Fire Department; Kimberly Bauer, for her unflagging support of local authors and literacy in New Brunswick schools; the Canada Council of the Arts for their ongoing support of Canadian artists and authors; my wonderful and witty editor, Penelope Jackson, for her eternal patience and encouragement; and, of course, my family and friends for their support, patience, and enthusiasm.
Thank you, all!